There I Find Joy

Strawberry Sands Book Four

Jessie Gussman

Published By: Jessie Gussman

Contents

Acknowledgements

Cover art by Kim Killion of The Killion Group

Editing by Heather Hayden

Narration by Jay Dyess

Author Services by CE Author Assistant

Listen to the unabridged audio for FREE performed by Jay Dyess on the Say with Jay channel on YouTube. Get early access to all of Jay's recordings and listen to Jessie's books before they're available to the general public, plus get daily Bible readings by Jay and bonus scenes by becoming a Say with Jay channel member .

Chapter 1

"Can I talk to you for a second, Luke?"

Luke set the bag of groceries that he had just picked up for his mother down on her kitchen table and looked her in the eye. "You know, when I was a kid, those words struck fear into my heart."

She laughed a little, but it was lacking her usual jovial nature, and his heart really did squeeze a little. Was there something wrong?

"Well, I guess this shouldn't strike fear into you, but this does have the potential to change your life."

"Mom. Just spit it out. Because you're scaring me." He said the words with a smile, but there was a note of seriousness behind them. Typically, she did not start their conversations like this. He was almost thirty years old and had been out of the house for years, although he still lived on the farm, in a small cottage on the upper side of the pasture.

He could look out the window and see horses grazing in the field. He'd grown up in this house and on this farm. Right along the shores of Lake Michigan. It had been a tough life. The grass wasn't exactly plentiful, and they had to work hard in order to have enough hay to feed the horses that they rented out to tourists so they could ride along the beach.

But he loved it. Loved the lake, loved the farm, and horses were in his blood.

He loved the town too, although sometimes it did get a little old, having everyone know everyone else's business.

Particularly Miss Heather, who was constantly trying to get him to marry her grand-daughter, Kristin. He'd taken to avoiding town completely, because it seemed like every time he went, Miss Heather figured it out through the grapevine and was there to waylay him somehow.

"This is about Becky." His mother twisted her hands in front of her, then turned toward the cupboard and pulled out a coffee mug. She didn't drink coffee, so he wasn't surprised when she pulled out a couple of the chocolate-covered espresso beans that she had become addicted to over the last few months and popped two in her mouth.

Becky was the orphan that the town had pretty much adopted. They had been shuffling her from house to house, everyone taking a turn at keeping her, while they figured out her foster situation.

Someone in the town was connected to someone at Blueberry Beach who had pulled a few strings at the state level to allow them to do things a bit differently.

Becky had run away from her original foster home because she wanted to be with her sister Rita, who was fostered by a couple in Strawberry Sands.

Everyone could sympathize with her, since Becky had nothing in the world except her sister.

Luke had taken his turn at keeping her for the day, while his mom had kept her for the night.

He and Becky had gone for a long ride along the beach, which Becky had seemed to love, then they'd eaten ice cream, and Becky had helped him take care of the horses. That was her normal job at the other horse stable in Strawberry Sands.

"Did they find a home for her?" he asked, wondering if he maybe needed some of those espresso beans, because his mother's face had not smoothed out.

"Kind of," his mother said, and he felt like she was hedging.

"What are you not telling me?" he asked, and he did reach over to the coffee mug she held and picked two beans out for himself.

He stuck them in his mouth, crunched down, and immediately regretted it. He had no idea what his mother saw in those things, but they tasted awful.

He walked over to the garbage can and spit them out.

His mother watched him, and he couldn't figure out whether the look in her eye was because she was annoyed that he wasted two of her beans, or if it was because she couldn't quite figure out how to tell him what she obviously was having trouble spitting out.

"Mom, whatever it is, I'll handle it. Just tell me."

"All right. I really don't know how else to say this. Becky enjoyed her time with you, and she wants you to be her dad."

He forgot all about the bitter taste which still clung to his tongue as he stared at his mother. "Me?" he managed to squeak out. Then he cleared his throat. "She wants me?"

That was so odd. His oldest brother Matt was in a stable relationship and already had a home and family. His sister Sunday already had a child. His mom was the kind of woman that every kid loved, and even his youngest sister Clara had just moved to Strawberry Sands with her boss, and they would soon be planning a wedding as well. He was the third child, a bit of a loose cannon, and he'd never really had even a steady girlfriend. He dated a few times, but he was terrible at dating, because he didn't focus on the things that everyone else thought was so important.

Plus, the whole town knew he had a long-standing feud with Kristin, the woman whose gram continuously tried to get him to marry her. And truth be told, he kind of enjoyed it.

He thought she did too.

Their animosity dated back to junior high and a fateful sailboat trip. Although, he figured he was probably the only one who still remembered that.

No, that wasn't true. Kristin wouldn't have forgotten either. They both thought they were going to die.

He shook those memories away and tried to focus on the issue at hand.

"Are you sure she didn't mean Matt? I mean, people get us confused." They were brothers, and they looked like it. He didn't know how many times in school he'd been called by Matt's name. Teachers who had had his older brother constantly forgot that Luke was a completely different person. Luke had gotten used to it, and he answered to his name or his brother's name. That was the most reasonable thing to do, rather than trying to correct everyone every time they got the name wrong.

"I'm sure. She talked about your horse ride and how much fun she had eating ice cream with you and that type of thing." His mother paused. And that's when Luke's stomach really started to dip. Apparently, Becky naming him as the man she wanted as her father was not the worst news his mother had to deliver.

"What are you not telling me?" he asked.

"Well, she named you as the father."

And that's when he figured it out. She had named a father *and* a mother.

"And?" he asked, thinking that it probably wasn't that bad. She probably chose one of his sisters, maybe Clara. Everyone loved Clara, and he would just have to share custody or something with her. That wouldn't be so terrible.

"And she wants Kristin to be her mother."

<h1 style="text-align:center">Chapter 2</h1>

Becky wanted him to be her father and Kristin to be her mother.

"But the kid doesn't really get to pick her parents, right?" he said, mostly because he was trying to hide the fact that he was horrified. There was no way he was going to co-parent with Kristin. Not with Miss Heather breathing down his neck. She would constantly be trying to find ways to put them together, and knowing Miss Heather, she'd lock them in a cell or something until he emerged with a ring on her finger. Or something like that.

He could almost see a Rapunzel-like scenario where they got trapped in a tower together. Of course, the only thing that even remotely resembled a tower was the lighthouse up the beach, where the old fellow who his mother looked after lived.

He tried to shove the fears of being trapped in a tower away. That was almost like being trapped on a sailboat in the middle of Lake Michigan, with a storm brewing and no way to get in touch with anyone on shore.

That had been the scariest time of his life.

This definitely rivaled that moment. The idea that someone wanted him to be their dad. He, who barely had his own life together, and then to top it off with the fact that they wanted Kristin, whom he hadn't talked to, other than to exchange insults with, in years.

"This is very unconventional, but considering Becky has already run away from home once, they really don't want to put her in juvie, because she's not a bad kid. They want to try to do what they can to help her grow up to be a productive member of society. And it helps that there's an anonymous liaison in Blueberry Beach. Someone who apparently has access to the system and insider pull. Anyway, they're working as hard as they can to get Becky settled with a couple, and when Becky told her caseworker that she wanted you and Kristin, the caseworker said that she was going to try to do everything in her power to get Becky what she wanted. Becky had given her word that she wouldn't run away if you two were her parents."

"Why not just Kristin?"

"Becky told her caseworker in no uncertain terms that a child needed a mom and dad."

"I can be the dad, and you could be the mom." He knew he sounded desperate, but he didn't know what else to do. He couldn't even talk to Kristin, let alone raise a child with her. That would also mean he would have to be around Miss Heather. He felt a shudder go through him.

"Apparently, she liked Kristin because they invited her sister to their house, and they baked cookies together. She enjoyed the older ladies that were there. She said that it was like having three grandmothers, when she hadn't ever even had one."

That made Luke's heart twist. The poor kid. Sure, his dad had split when he was just a kid, but he had his mom, who was the best mom in the entire world, raise him, and he couldn't have had a happier childhood.

He barely remembered his dad, and he didn't remember missing him when he left.

He did remember longing for a dad though. Wondering why his dad didn't love him, and wondering why his parents couldn't just live together like everyone else's.

He hated that Becky had that too. He wouldn't wish that on anyone. And the fact that there was something he could do to help it didn't sit easy with him either. Especially since he didn't want to.

"I know that's sad, but it seems to me like she'd be better off with either Kristin or me, but having the two of us together would just be stress and strain, and probably a lot of arguing."

"You duck out every time she's anywhere around, because you're afraid of her grand-mother. You need to get over that." His mother used her no-nonsense tone. The one she used when he was a kid and was trying to get out of doing something he didn't want to do, like eating his peas or brushing his teeth. It was the kind of tone where she said he was going to do it or else.

He didn't want to argue with his mom, but he also didn't want to be anywhere near Kristin's gram.

He opened his mouth, but his mom beat him.

"I understand that Kristin is not the problem."

He gave a jerk of his head. Kristin wasn't his favorite person. They always ended up fighting anytime they were around each other, which was how they ended up on that sailboat, out in the middle of Lake Michigan. And almost died.

"But are you really going to let your fear of some elderly lady, who really wants the best for her granddaughter, keep you from possibly giving a little girl a better life?"

His mom always asked the questions that cut right to the heart of the matter.

She didn't have to tell him that he was being selfish. After all, people had invested in him, which is why he turned out the way he had. His mom had been a single mom, but the small town of Strawberry Sands had rallied around her and helped her raise her children.

Anyone who had relatives staying had them stay at their bed-and-breakfast. They bought hay from them, rented horses, and supported their business however they could. They helped them get their farmwork done until he and his brothers were old enough to do it themselves, and he could remember more than once people dropping off meals when their family had been working all day, and their mom hadn't had a chance to make anything.

If it hadn't been for the whole town of Strawberry Sands rallying around them, neither he nor any of his siblings would have had the life they did.

He owed the town a lot.

Maybe this was how the Lord wanted him to pay it back.

Lord, I know I'm not supposed to hoard the things You give me. But I'm supposed to give freely, so You can give me more. I understand that. But, Lord? A little girl? Kristin? And come on, Miss Heather?

His mom fished another chocolate-covered espresso bean out of her mug and put it in her mouth.

Her face had smoothed out. It was obvious that she knew he was wavering.

Maybe it was even more obvious that she had faith in him. That she believed he was going to make the right decision. Yeah, that's what he could read on her face. Maybe that was what convinced him more than anything: she had faith that he was going to do the right thing. That he was going to give back and let go of his cushy, uncomplicated life.

That he would wade in, however that looked, and involve himself with Kristin and, more importantly, with Becky. Putting up with Miss Heather in order to do so.

"I wish you wouldn't look at me like that." His tone sounded a little bit belligerent. Like he was sixteen instead of almost thirty.

"Like what?" his mother said, total innocence on her face.

"Like you know I'm going to do the right thing. That puts a lot of pressure on me."

"Pressure to do the right thing?" she asked with her brows lifted.

He grunted, because the way she asked made it sound like she was asking him what was wrong with that. Which of course was a reasonable question.

"I guess Kristin and I can co-parent, if it comes to that." He couldn't believe the foster care system was going to allow this to happen. It had to be more than unusual. But then again, he didn't think that they probably lost a lot of kids, finding them living homeless and working at a stable in order to earn money to eat, just so they could be with their sibling.

Becky was obviously an unusual case.

"Co-parent? Do you really think that is something that would work?" his mother asked, and there was a bit of derision in her tone.

People did it. Of course they did. Sometimes they didn't have a choice.

Life wasn't perfect, after all. It wasn't like he would consider getting married.

"Maybe you should consider getting married to Kristin."

If he'd had a drink in his mouth, he would have spit it out.

"What?" His tone said it all.

"Luke. You and Kristin have been attracted to each other forever. I don't know what happened that day on the lake, but I hated to see you allow it to come between the two of you and drive you so completely apart." His mother stopped short of telling him that he should marry her again. "Why don't you just go and talk to her?"

His mother looked at him with lifted brows, again with confidence on her face that said she knew he was going to do the right thing.

Getting married to someone he could barely stand was definitely not the right thing.

She had a point with Becky. He needed to give back. Anytime God asked for something from him, he should give it willingly. After all, God had given him so very much.

But it was one thing to offer a home to a child and to co-parent with someone. It was a completely different story to pledge the rest of his life to someone he wasn't in love with.

After all, wasn't that the main requirement of marriage? To be in love?

Somehow that didn't quite sound right. It sounded like what the world told him, but God never said a person had to be in love in order to get married. He just said a person had to love. There apparently was a difference between falling and choosing.

He just hadn't been interested in doing either, so he stayed away from marriage.

"I'll go talk to her." The words were out of his mouth before he thought about them. After all, going to Kristin's house meant potentially seeing Miss Heather. Seeing Miss Heather meant being attacked by a woman who was determined to get her grippy claws into him and make him marry her granddaughter.

In a small town like Strawberry Sands, it was difficult to avoid her, but he'd managed to do it, having an almost perfect track record for the time he'd been in Strawberry Sands. Just a few little slip-ups on his end.

"I think she'll be reasonable. And I think both of you will have Becky's best interest at heart. And there's a possibility that Rita could be moved into your home, if you're willing to adopt them both. Rita is just being fostered right now."

Rita was Becky's sister and the reason Becky had run away from her foster home. The little he knew about the foster care system said that if a family was willing to take siblings, they got precedence over a family who wasn't.

If he was going to take one, he might as well take two, but he didn't know how Kristin felt about it.

Maybe she would go running at the thought of co-parenting with him. He couldn't begin to think that they might actually consider marriage. That was impossible.

Wasn't it?

Chapter 3

Kristin flipped an egg and tried unsuccessfully not to listen to the conversation behind her.

"We have to waylay him! He can't know what hit him!"

"Maybe we could do a sneak attack, Heather? Like, we could accidentally break a toilet, and he'd have to come fix it. Then we could lock them in the bathroom together and not let them out until he asks her on a date!"

Why was she thinking of allowing Miss Daisy to come live with her? She already had enough issues with her gram and Miss Alma and Miss Joyce. She should have known that Miss Daisy would join them in their "matchmaking" attempts, although that sounded more like attempted kidnapping than matchmaking.

"That's brilliant! Now I know why God had you move in with us!"

Move in? Kristin froze. It was true that she had several spare bedrooms in this behemoth of a house, and it was also true that she could use the extra income, since she didn't have a job other than taking care of her gram, but it was not true that she wanted to be ganged up on by four old ladies who had nothing better to do than to try to set her up with any man who breathed and could walk—or crawl—down the sidewalk in front of her house. Last week, they had tried to set her up with a man who was sixty if he was a day.

"Guys. Has it ever occurred to any of you that maybe I'm happy being single?"

She knew that line wouldn't work, and of course, it didn't. It only started the conversation about how much better off she would be when she was married.

She allowed the chatter to go in one ear and out the other. Really, if she didn't have to watch her gram to make sure she wasn't going to "accidentally" lock Kristin in a bathroom somewhere, she would be perfectly happy. She lived in the best town in the world, right by the most beautiful lake God created, her gram was in good health, and so was she. She had enough money to pay her bills and buy groceries, and really, life was good.

As she flipped the last egg out of the skillet, she thought she heard a knock at the door, but she couldn't be sure with the chatter of the ladies behind her.

Turning the skillet off and moving it off the burner, she left the kitchen without them noticing and walked to the front door, just to check.

Opening the door, she was shocked to see Luke Landry, who could almost be called her nemesis, standing on the porch, one hand in his pocket, one leaning against a big post, his face turned toward the lake like he wanted to be anywhere but there.

"Luke?" She tried not to sound like she hated him. She didn't, of course. It was just that her gram had pushed her toward him so forcefully that he'd started avoiding her rather obviously, to the point where he physically ran away from her if he saw her, and a girl couldn't help getting a little piqued over something like that.

He startled, and then immediately his eyes flew behind her. "Where's your gram?" he whispered, like he wasn't standing on her porch in broad daylight.

"She's eating a big, strong man for breakfast, and you're probably next. Are you sure it's safe to stand this close to me?"

Her words didn't make him relax. More because he was still worried about her gram coming out with a ring and the preacher than he was about getting eaten for breakfast, she was sure, but still.

"Okay, I'll be quick." He was still whispering, and he crept closer, like her gram could hear him taking a normal step. "You know Becky, the little girl with no home?"

"Yeah?" She'd loved her time with Becky, even though it had made her long for a husband and children of her own.

"She's decided who she wants as parents."

Kristin stared at him with her mouth open. She wasn't sure if she was more surprised that Becky got to "choose" her parents, and how did that happen, anyway? Or if she was more surprised that it was Luke who was telling her. Or even that anyone thought she needed to be told.

"Okay?" she finally said, sounding like she was asking all the questions she couldn't figure out how to ask. "Why are you telling me?"

"Because…" He paused, as though gathering up his nerve. "She chose us."

Kristin stood staring at Luke. "What did you say?"

"Do you mind coming out and taking a walk with me?" Luke said, peering behind her shoulder nervously.

She almost rolled her eyes, but she knew her gram could be quite a pill at times.

It was tempting to say something sarcastic, but instead, she tried to show compassion. "Sometimes she drives me crazy too," she said with a little lift of her shoulder as she pulled the door shut behind her.

His brows went up a bit, like he hadn't been expecting her to admit even that much.

Surely he knew that living with her was even harder than putting up with her once in a while around town?

Also, he had to know that her gram was the only family she had left. She could hardly turn her back on her, and she couldn't do anything but love her. After all, it was the world who only loved the easy people. Christians were supposed to be different. Christians were supposed to love the hard people too.

Though no one could fault Kristin for not loving her family.

As she came closer, Luke backed away, adjusting his cowboy hat on his head, as his square-toe cowboy boots found the step and stepped down.

He waited at the bottom of the stairs for her, and she fell into step beside him. Without talking, they walked toward the lake.

Up on the hill, horses grazed on either side of the town, their manes blowing gently in the wind, their calm unconcern for anything but the next mouthful of grass somehow easing the tight ball her stomach had become.

"I was just as shocked. Mom hit me with that just a little bit ago, and I couldn't believe it."

"Your mom told you?"

He nodded. "I'm not sure who she heard it from. I honestly didn't have the presence of mind to ask, although she said there was someone in Blueberry Beach who had some pull at the state level and was probably influencing what is very much an unconventional way to handle foster children."

"I'll say. I've never heard of a foster child getting to choose their parents."

"Me either."

"You told your mom that we weren't going to do it?"

"No. She... She looked at me the way moms do sometimes."

"I guess I don't know about that." She had been raised by an aunt, who had passed away.

"I'm sorry. I forgot."

"No problem." Most people forgot. Or didn't understand. Because most people had parents. At least one. Although, she supposed there were more people like her than anyone wanted to admit. People who didn't exactly have the traditional homelife of mom and dad in the home with them.

"I guess just the way she said it reminded me that God had given me a lot and that I should be willing to give whatever He asks in return."

"Even if that means parenting a little girl? Which will change your whole life?"

"I know. But I owe Him at least that much and so much more."

She lifted her chin and looked away toward the horses again. Even if she hadn't had parents, God had provided an aunt to raise her. He provided her gram. He provided a lot.

"Maybe God provides what He does so we can enjoy it and live a pleasant life."

"And maybe He gives us what He does so we can give it away and He can give us more."

That sounded more like the Lord. Wanting to know if they would be a blessing with what they had been given, a good steward, so He could bless them and trust them with even more. She thought about the parable of the talents, where some people invested their talents and earned more, while the people who just kept the talents hidden for themselves didn't get anything extra, other than a condemnation from the master when he returned.

"If we were to do that..." She couldn't even believe she was considering it. "What would that look like?"

"I'm not sure." Luke scuffed his boots on the sidewalk, like he was thinking, before he shoved his hands in his pockets and looked off in the distance at the horses and the lake, lifting his head to the breeze.

"I guess this is the first time in years that we've actually had a conversation that didn't involve insults and anger." She supposed she shouldn't have said that. Shouldn't have pointed out their weaknesses toward each other. But she couldn't really help it. After all, it was the truth. She hadn't talked to Luke in years. Not like this.

"I know. That's mostly my fault. I'm sorry."

Did Luke just apologize to her?

"I'm sorry about my gram. I... I understand that she can be..."

"Overwhelming? Like a shark? Like a bulldog? A pirate with a hook hand and—"

"Hey! That's enough. You don't have to be a jerk."

"I wasn't saying anything that wasn't true."

"It might be true to you, but she's my gram."

"I don't care whose gram she is, she's a nosy old biddy who's pretty much attacked me every time she sees me."

"She's doing it because she loves me."

"Well, she doesn't have any consideration for anyone else."

She stopped, putting her hands on her hips and glaring at Luke. The idea that anyone thought that they could actually get along long enough to...

Couldn't they?

The anger drained out of her. Couldn't she get along with him for the sake of a child? Possibly two children?

"I'm sorry. You're right. She's annoying and all of those other things you said." She looked down, contrite. Who was she to get angry? He wasn't saying anything but the truth. Even if it did hurt.

"No. I'm sorry. I... I guess I got a little carried away. You're right. She only means the best. Maybe she even thinks..."

Kristin waited. But he didn't finish.

"Thinks what?" she finally prompted.

He shook his head. "I was just going to say maybe she was thinking she was doing the best thing for me too. After all, if she loves you, she probably thinks whoever gets you is getting quite the catch."

His words hurt. Because he wasn't saying that they *were* getting a catch, he was just saying that Gram thought they were getting a catch. There was a big difference. Obviously, he didn't think she was a catch.

She tried not to allow that to bother her. Even as she thought that Luke was quite a catch. He was a hardworking man who wasn't terrible to look at. He had character and integrity, he was honest and upright. He would take care of his family, he was respectful to his mother. After all, from what he said, that was the whole reason that he was here. Because his mother wanted him to try.

And God did too. She could respect a man who was doing what God wanted him to do. She could admit that a man like that would be a man worth having.

Even if he didn't think that she was a woman worth having.

"So what should we do? Co-parent?"

"That's not what my mom suggested."

"Your mom had an idea?"

Everyone knew Mrs. Landry was a wise woman who'd managed to hold the farm together after her husband left, raise all of her children, and run a successful bed-and-breakfast. Kristin wasn't quite sure how she managed to do all that, but anyone who could was a person worth listening to. If Mrs. Landry had advice, Kristin would be taking it.

"She suggested we get married."

Or not.

"She suggested what?" Kristin asked, sure she had misheard. Mrs. Landry wouldn't suggest that. She knew that Luke and Kristin couldn't manage to get along for five minutes. Look at them. They were fighting before they'd even made it to the lake.

"I know. I had the same reaction. But it made sense to me. After all, no sacrifice would be too great to do what God wants me to do."

"I guess I kind of resent the idea that being married to me would be considered a sacrifice." She mumbled that, annoyed with him. And annoyed with herself for being annoyed to begin with.

"Sorry. I guess it's a sacrifice for you too. So the sacrifice that both of us would have to make wouldn't be too big, not for God. Not for a little girl, and there would be potential to adopt her sister, Rita, who is just in foster care right now. The state always puts a premium on keeping siblings together, and Becky really wants to be with her sister."

"So you're suggesting that you and I get married so that the two sisters can stay together?"

"I wasn't suggesting it, I was just telling you what my mom said."

"And you're willing?" She lifted her brow and looked him straight in the eye.

He looked over her shoulder, presumably at the horses that were grazing behind her.

She turned her head and looked at the lake. Wild and beautiful, and somehow calm, calm enough for her to draw strength from. Knowing that God was in control. As big and great and mighty as the lake was, as still and peaceful as it was, God was bigger, God was greater, God was mightier. God was even more peaceful, and He was even more still.

"I'm willing."

He didn't look at her as he spoke but kept his eyes over her shoulder. Like he was willing to die, truly sacrifice himself, if that's what God wanted.

One part of her admired that, and another part of her screamed that she needed to say no and say it now.

"Do you think we can be happy together?" She didn't even want to question whether or not they could learn to love each other. The question was whether they could learn to tolerate each other.

"I think happiness is a choice."

She'd heard that.

A Bible verse, one that she hadn't thought of in a long time, popped through her mind. "The joy of the Lord is my strength."

His lips curved up a little, and his eyes moved to hers. "Exactly."

Could they find joy together?

Chapter 4

"The Strawberry Festival was great for your business, Chi," Kristin said as she helped Charlotte put the stools upside down on top of the bar so they could mop the floor.

Charlotte appreciated Kristin's help.

"Where did you say Griff went?" Kristin asked as she set the last stool up.

"He went to Chicago. He didn't say why." She was curious herself. Griff never took off work. Ever. And yet he told her this morning that he wasn't going to be there to help her clean up because he had to leave right after they closed.

She didn't ask why, and honestly, at the time she hadn't thought to. She'd been looking for James, the lawyer who often showed up on Thursdays. Today he hadn't.

But it had gotten her thinking. Griff was the backbone of the diner. Maybe Charlotte started it, but Griff was the cook, and people were coming, from far and wide, for a taste of the strawberry treats he made. They were doing quite a great business, but without Griff, she wasn't sure she would be successful. She hadn't exactly realized that until today.

"I'm so glad you're here. With Griff gone, there is a lot of work to do to close up." So far, it had just been Griff and her working the diner. But if they continued to be as busy as what they had been, she was going to have to hire people. Both of them were working way more than people should, and while Griff didn't seem to be any worse for the wear, she was exhausted.

"I don't mind at all. I needed to do something to keep my mind off of things."

"Is your gram attacking people again? Forcing men into your house in order to look you over as a potential bride?" They joked about it often, how aggressive her gram was in trying to get her married. She was so aggressive that she scared men off. Which was too bad, because Kristin was a really great person.

"Actually, it's not my gram this time. Although, I do have someone who…might *sacrifice* in order to marry me."

Kristin's voice held derision, which made Charlotte stop in the midst of sweeping up the floor. "Sacrifice? What are you talking about?"

With as little fanfare as possible, Kristin told her about Becky and how she had decided that she wanted Kristin and Luke as parents.

"That's crazy."

"That's exactly what I said."

And then she said what Luke's mother had said about the state possibly allowing it and about what Mrs. Landry had also said about getting married.

"She suggested you get married?" Chi couldn't stop herself from saying, with as much disbelief as it was possible for a person to have in her voice.

"I know! That's how I felt about it. I couldn't believe it. But that's the truth."

"And of course, you dismissed that right away. You and Luke can't even stand to be in the same town together."

"I know. We walked from my house and didn't even make it to the lake before we were fighting."

"That sounds normal."

"I know. He was insulting Gram, and I couldn't stop myself from getting upset with him."

"And you stormed away, of course."

"No. He apologized. So then I found myself apologizing, too."

"Wow. That's interesting."

"I know, right?" Kristin said, bringing the bucket of soapy water around so she could start scrubbing where Chi had already swept.

"So what did you guys decide to do?" Then a thought occurred to her. "Are you already married?"

"No!" Kristin sighed. "We just kind of agreed to think about it for a little bit, and then he walked away and I walked back to the house."

"And so what are you thinking?"

"I'm thinking that... Sometimes God asks us to do crazy things. But more than that, God has given me so much. That's part of the reason when Gram asked if her friends could move in with her, I said yes. After all, I have a huge house, it has eight bedrooms, and we're only using five of them. I've got three more. So... I could have two little girls and...a husband?" She broke off with an uncomfortable laugh.

"Well, that's a good way to look at it, I guess." Chi wasn't sure she would see things the same way. After all, the idea of marrying someone she didn't love was not appealing, but she supposed that love was a choice. And the feeling that a lot of people associated as love didn't last. Maybe that was why so many marriages didn't last. But she couldn't stop herself from wanting that feeling. After all, didn't everyone want love?

"I've been thinking about it all day. It makes sense. The idea that God has given so much to me, so what am I giving in return? I mean, if everything in life is about serving God and bringing glory to Him, then giving another room in my house, giving my whole life, shouldn't be too much, should it?"

"I suppose not. After all, Jesus gave his life for us. Isn't that what He requires in return? Our lives?"

"I don't know that it's a requirement, but it seems like a fit payment. If you owe someone a debt, don't you try to repay it? After all, you don't let someone just do nice things for you without ever trying to do nice things in return."

That was true. Kristin was here, helping her clean up, but she would do something for Kristin in return, probably sit with her gram some evening so Kristin could go to the gym or take a horse ride.

They had been switching off and on like that for months. Neither one of them keeping track, just making sure that they helped each other.

She couldn't outgive Jesus, but she didn't want her relationship to be so unequal.

"How do you feel about Becky? You watched her."

"I loved her! We even had her sister there. And she made the ladies laugh. Gram had a blast that day, and they were talking about having her back so they could make bread."

"Did Becky enjoy it?"

"She did."

They talked a little more about the fun they'd had that day, but Chi was still thinking about unequal relationships.

She had been thinking about how much she owed Griff and how the diner wouldn't be nearly as successful as what it was if it weren't for him. But he barely got paid anything. Just a little over minimum wage, and she really couldn't afford to pay more.

She hadn't paid a lot of attention to him either. He was just there. Always with his strawberry recipes, trying something out.

Come to think of it, he added new recipes to the diner as well. He often had a weekly special, and people would come back night after night to get more. Word would spread, and by Friday and Saturday night, the diner would be full of people coming to get Griff's special.

And they'd take home his dessert.

Thirty minutes later, they finished mopping floors and stood at the door.

"I really appreciate you helping me tonight. We cut the time in half at least. And it's much more fun to do it with a friend."

It kept her mind off of what Griff might be doing, and even more than that, it had kept her mind off of the fact that James hadn't shown. It wasn't the first time he hadn't kept his word. Or that he had said he was going to be somewhere and not even called to let her know that his plans had changed.

The next time she saw him, he'd have some great stories. A client who had an emergency, a family member that he needed to take care of. Always his excuses were plausible, but the fact that he hadn't told her that he wasn't going to make it, but just didn't show, still irked.

At the same time, she never had anyone who was so successful, rich, suave, handsome, and everything she dreamed about as a little girl, interested in her.

She didn't want to give him too hard of a time, because she didn't want to run him off. He was her best hope of... She wanted to say getting out of this little town, but she liked it here.

Gaining some social acceptability, but she actually had that too.

She just...wanted to know that someone like him could or would want to be with someone like her.

She had been tempted more than once to show up at his office in Chicago. Most of the time, he claimed that he had to work and hadn't been able to make it. She just...wanted to see.

There was a part of her that didn't quite believe him. Most of her told that part of her to shut up. But it was the loudest part and told her that maybe if she made a trip to Chicago, her eyes might be opened in a way she wouldn't like but that would be beneficial to her in the long run.

So far, she hadn't done it.

"Have you decided what you're going to do?" she asked, trying to turn away from the thoughts in her head. Trying to be a good friend. Trying to support Kristin and whatever she decided.

"What would you do if you were me?"

"Luke is a good guy. He is respectable in this town. He's a hard worker. I mean, he doesn't have a whole lot of money or anything, but... He'd probably be a good dad." For her, she wanted someone with money. Someone who didn't just have respectability but had a good, high-paying job. Someone who could take care of her. Someone she could look up to and admire for his accomplishments in the world.

There was a nagging part of her that said none of the things that she wanted was important, but they were all things that she'd grown up being told she needed, and after the things she'd gotten into, she almost craved them.

"But you wouldn't marry him?" Kristin prompted.

Would she?

"Even to give a little girl and her sister a home?"

"I don't think he's right for me, but I've seen you two together a couple of times, and if you could manage to not fight, I think you might get along pretty well." That was the honest truth. "But if I were you, I wouldn't take advice from me. What do I know? Look at me." She looked around the diner. It was dingy, and she barely made a living, paying her one employee less than a living wage.

"But you're happy here. And you make people happy. You and Griff. You're a great team. You're the face of the diner, always with a kind word, and he's back there creating all kinds of recipes that have people coming back for more." Kristin smiled. "It's getting quite a reputation." Then her brows drew down. "Have you guys decided whether or not you're moving to the location at the edge of town? The one where you have the patio overlooking the lake and the horses?"

"It's almost finalized. Next month this time, we could be up and running over there." She wasn't sure how long it would take to move, but the wheels had already started turning, and she figured she might as well go with it. Unless of course, James asked her to marry him. If that happened, she'd close the diner in a heartbeat and run off with him. And she wanted to think that could happen any day.

He had hinted around at it; he'd also hinted around about wanting her to go on an overnight trip with him. She'd been tempted. Even though she'd sworn those kinds of things off. Still, she kind of felt like if she did that, he'd be more inclined to marry her.

"I'm happy to hear it! I can't wait until it's there. I think it will be even more popular than it is here. And that's such a beautiful location. Not very far away, but that patio is awesome."

"It'll be popular with the tourists in summer, that's for sure." She had to agree. Part of her wanted to dig in and put everything she had into the diner. Part of her was holding out hope that James would propose, and she could leave the cares and the worries of the diner behind and become the socialite she'd always wanted to be.

Still... What about Griff?

She tried to push that thought aside. It wasn't like he couldn't find something else to do. She didn't think he had been a short-order cook to begin with. He'd just seen her one day, knew she needed help, parked his bike, and moved in.

He could move out just as easily.

"I'm sorry I can't help you more," she said as Kristin put a hand on the door.

"No. I think just talking about it made me feel better. I am... I'm leaning toward saying yes. After all, there are a lot of worse people out there."

"There are. And there are worse reasons to get married." For sure.

"That's true. I love the idea of being a family. I just don't... I'm not sure that I love the idea of being a family with Luke. He..."

"You think he's handsome anyway."

"It doesn't really matter what he looks like. I'd take integrity over looks all day long."

Chi wasn't sure that's what she wanted. Although she knew that was the smart way to go. Why couldn't she live her life with intelligence, rather than with dreams?

"It sounds to me like you're going to make the right decision."

"I'm gonna pray about it."

"I'll do that too." And she would. And while she was at it, she'd pray for herself. After all, maybe there were lingering doubts about James for a reason.

Chapter 5

"Rodney? Are you awake?"

Rodney kept his eyes closed and his breathing steady. The last thing he wanted to do was talk to Becky after she slipped into his room and crawled on top of the covers, taking the blanket that he kept on the chair for her and tucking it around her.

He'd almost locked his door. That would keep her out, except, knowing Becky, she would have pounded on the sliding door until he got out of bed and opened it for her.

"Rodney!" she hissed, shoving her pointy elbow into his stomach.

He grunted. "What do you want, Beckpet?" He used the nickname he had given her, the one she hated.

"Shut up, Dixie. I just wanted to talk to you. I know you're not asleep."

"How do you know that?"

"Because you're never asleep when I crawl in."

"Maybe I'm tired today. I had a hard tennis practice." Actually, today hadn't been tennis day at all. He had walked down to the lake and gone for a swim. He wasn't technically allowed to go into the lake by himself, but since he'd seen his dad with his hand on the waitress's thigh, he hadn't really cared too much about his parents' rules.

What was the point in following their rules when they didn't follow rules?

"What's wrong with you? For the last three weeks, you've been a bear." Becky sounded put out, and it almost made him smile. It was like there wasn't anyone else in the world who was allowed to be grumpy except for her.

"It's your imagination, Beckpet. Go to sleep."

"I told you. I want to talk to you. I need to."

He didn't want to talk. Not to her, not to anyone. He just wanted to unsee what he had seen, only he couldn't. His dad was a slimeball.

"Then talk," he said, and there wasn't much charity in his voice.

"I'm not going to talk to you if you're going to be a jerk. I don't understand why."

He felt bad. Becky hadn't had too many people be kind to her in her life. Even if his dad was a slimeball, at least he had a place to sleep and didn't have to sneak into someone else's house for food or to have a bed. Not yet anyway. Of course, if his parents got divorced, he wasn't likely going to be destitute. It was just going to...explode his world. Although, he supposed instead of being depressed about a possible divorce, he should be shocked that his parents had managed to stay together for almost eighteen years. A lot of people didn't.

Along those lines, he wondered if this wasn't the first affair his dad had had, and his mom just turned a blind eye to it. Maybe she was busy having affairs of her own.

He never thought along those lines. Not until he saw that hand on that thigh.

"I'm sorry. I haven't been a very good friend."

"You've been a great friend. You've just been preoccupied lately. What's the problem?"

"No problem." He wanted to turn the conversation from him. He wasn't going to tell Becky what he'd seen. He wasn't going to tell anyone. He was going to do everything in his power to pretend it hadn't happened. "Tell me what you came here for. What you're so excited about." He smiled a little. Becky couldn't hide her emotions. Whatever she was feeling was what she was.

"I think I might be getting a home. And I think I might be getting it with my sister!" She squealed, and he had to shush her. Just because his dad was cheating didn't mean that he wouldn't be in a huge amount of trouble if someone found Becky in his bed. Even if the covers were between them, and even if he didn't really invite her. He was the one who had left the door unlocked, although that wouldn't really matter either. Nothing would matter, other than their ages and the fact that she was in his bed.

"How did that happen?" he asked, shoving the idea of him getting in trouble aside.

"I just said that's what I wanted. I liked being at Miss Kristin's house, because her grandma and her friends got my sister, and we spent the day baking in their kitchen. We made the most delicious cookies, remember?"

"I remember. They were good. But you haven't made any more, so I'm not sure if you actually made them or if you stole them from someone."

"Stop it. I don't steal what I don't need."

He shouldn't have teased her about it. She didn't like stealing; she didn't like doing anything that was illegal. It bothered her, and he liked that. Liked that she had a conscience, unlike a lot of adults he knew. Including his own dad.

"I'll make you more. Just as soon as I have a home."

"Did she say she was going to adopt you?"

"I don't want just her. I said I wanted a mom *and* a dad."

"But she's not married. Is she?" He scrunched up his nose, trying to remember who Miss Kristin was. He spent more time in Strawberry Sands than his parents did. Scratch that. He thought he spent more time in Strawberry Sands than his parents did, but, well, his dad was obviously going there without anyone's knowledge. At least without his knowledge. His dad always said that Strawberry Sands was just a hick town and that Blueberry Beach was where it was at.

"No. But I chose a man for her. It's one that she actually likes, and he likes her, it's just when they get together, they always fight. Mostly because Kristin's gram is always trying to get them together, and that makes Luke want to run away."

"Luke Landry? He's related to Matt who owns the other stable in Strawberry Sands?"

"Yeah. That's the one. He helps with the horses, making hay. He's really nice, and when I spent the day with him, we went on a horse ride up the beach, had a picnic, and we went swimming in the water. It was cold, and I didn't stay in very long, but he didn't rush me at all. He taught me how to do the backstroke. And he even said that if we did it again, we'd take the horses in our swimming suits and ride them bareback into the water. He said that horses could swim."

"I don't know if I trust him," Rodney said dubiously. He didn't know about horses and swimming. But Becky was a pretty good judge of character, and if she liked Luke, he was probably a man worth liking. Still, he didn't like the idea of Becky being in the water over her head bareback on a horse. "Maybe you trust too easily."

"I don't trust at all, and you know it," she spat out, sounding sour again. His mood was rubbing off on her. He hated that and worked a little harder to try to pull his soul out of the dungeon where it had been since he'd seen his dad feeling up that waitress.

"If they're not married, I don't understand how you're going to have a home and family. What are they going to do? Shuffle you back and forth between their houses?"

"I said I wasn't doing it unless I had a mom and a dad. People want me to have a home so bad, they might be willing to do something that crazy. And they really don't understand that it's for their best interests. Those two were made for each other."

"Now you're a matchmaker."

"Shut up, Dixie. I know what I know, and I'm sure about this."

She might be. Becky had a tendency to be smarter than what he gave her credit for. She had street smarts. A lot more than he did.

After all, how dumb could a guy be? His own dad was cheating on his mom, right under his nose practically, and he hadn't even realized.

He was under the impression that the day he'd seen his dad's hand on that waitress's thigh wasn't the first time his hand had been there. No. It was way too confident for that to be the first time.

"You're sure about what? That you want them for your parents? Or that they're going to get together because of you?"

"That everything is going to work out." Becky said those words softly, and there was a wishful note in her tone that he didn't often get to hear. She was hoping everything worked out, but she was saying that she thought it would just to project confidence, because that was Becky. A lot of bluster, a lot of bluff, a lot of swagger, but underneath, she was just a little girl who wanted a family with her sister more than anything. Wanted someone to love her.

Wasn't that what they all wanted?

Rodney had been thinking about that a lot since he'd seen what he had with his dad. It had shaken his world and made him feel less secure. And even though he had trouble reconciling the fact that his dad claimed to be a Christian and yet acted the way he had, he also knew that God hadn't changed. God was still there. God still loved him.

Then why did He allow him to see what he had? Why was He allowing this trial?

Maybe it was so that he would stop putting his hope in his earthly father and turn toward his heavenly father.

He didn't feel ready to do that though.

But he could have been like Becky, who had no earthly father to put any hope in. Let alone an earthly mother. She had nothing. Nothing except for him, and the hope of a possible family. And the knowledge of God who loved her, even though he wasn't sure she believed it at times either.

"You know, even if you never get a family. Even if you never live with your sister again, God loves you."

"I've heard that. Not sure I believe it though. What makes you think that there even is a God?"

"What makes you think there isn't?" he countered.

"Where is He?" she asked simply.

"He's right here," he answered just as simply.

"I can't see him."

"There's a lot of things we can't see. I can't see your sister, but I know she's in Strawberry Sands tonight too."

"True," Becky conceded, and it was a big concession, because Becky didn't usually give ground in an argument. "I guess if God allows me to have a family, I just might believe in Him."

"I don't think it works like that. I think you're supposed to believe first."

"I suppose that's the way it should be. But I don't know that I've seen Him the way other people have. I hear about love and goodness and all that stuff, but that comes from people who have a home and family."

"And maybe you'll have one one day. Or maybe you'll grow up knowing how important it is for a kid to have one, and you'll make sure that a bunch of kids get a home and family, because you know what it's like to not have one."

She was quiet for a while. "I suppose. That sounds nice. I think I'd like to do that. But I need to marry somebody who's going to make a lot of money so I can afford to stay home and take care of all the kids."

"I'll find someone for you," he promised. After all, he knew a lot of rich people. He could find someone who could like a scrappy thing like Becky. Actually, he could imagine a lot of men would be better off with someone like Becky beside him. Especially if it were her goal in life to have a family. Because if she made it so that that's what she wanted, that's what she would make sure she had.

He grinned a little with the thought. Somebody would be getting a tornado when they got Becky.

"I hope you get your family," he said, thinking about the irony of him losing his just as Becky got hers.

"Me too," she said, and he could hear the smile in her voice as she snuggled down beside him.

He'd been a little angry at God. Not that it was God's fault that his dad was cheating on his mom, but he supposed God was a good one for him to take his anger out on, even though it was undeserved.

He started out his prayer with an apology. Then, after he'd been sincere in his regret about giving God the silent treatment, he asked God for two simple things. One was that Becky would get her family, complete with a mom, dad, and sister. And the second was that what he saw in the diner would turn out to be nothing.

He had a feeling that God wasn't going to answer both of those prayers. The thought came to him—what if only one could be answered? Which one would he choose? To keep his world together, or to give Becky a chance at having a happy family?

It didn't take him long to think about that. And he prayed once more for Becky.

Chapter 6

Luke sat on the front porch of his beachside cottage. To the right, he could see horses grazing on the hill. Straight in front of him, Lake Michigan stretched out to where it met the sky on the horizon.

The waves were kicking up a little higher since he'd come in for lunch. A storm was brewing. The gentle breeze had turned into sharp gusts. They carried a little bit of water spray and a slight chill, despite the hot summer day.

He loved storms that came off the lake.

The horses didn't seem bothered but grazed placidly. They'd been around long enough to know that storms came and they went, and eating was more important.

Luke put the last of his tuna salad sandwich in his mouth and chewed thoughtfully.

He wasn't sure exactly what to do. He'd all but asked Kristin to marry him. Or offered, or whatever. He wasn't even sure himself. He said he was willing. He'd do it for Becky. She'd only spent one day with him, but she pretty much had the entire town wrapped around her little fingers, and pretty much anyone in town would do anything for her. That included him.

But if Kristin wasn't willing, there wasn't a whole lot he could do.

Funny, because when he first thought of it, he had been the reluctant one. Now he found himself in the odd position of trying to figure out how to convince someone he didn't know very well, and hadn't even thought he liked, to marry him.

And he had to do it while avoiding her gram.

As he sat there, a horse and rider came into view from the south. He watched them for a little bit, finally recognizing his youngest brother, Ryan.

Ryan had spent some time on the rodeo circuit, winning just enough to entice him to keep trying.

He finally came back home just a few weeks ago and was settling back into the routine of work on the farm.

Luke figured Ryan still had a bit of an itch, and he wasn't sure he was going to stick this time. Of all his brothers, and sisters for that matter, Ryan was the one with the most wanderlust. He was the one who liked to have action and friends and be constantly in the middle of everything.

He expected Ryan to just ride by, but maybe Ryan had seen him sitting on the porch, because he turned his horse and rode up, stopping by the front steps and not dismounting.

Luke didn't bother to take his feet down off the railing where he had them propped.

"Howdy. Nice afternoon for a ride. If you want to get wet," he said with a grin, glancing at the sky with clouds that boiled. They had turned from the innocuous-looking white to a more ominous, concerning gray.

"I'm down for a storm anytime. Bring it," Ryan said with a smirk.

"Don't think I'd go up against the Almighty like that."

"The storm isn't God," Ryan said casually, one hand resting on the pommel of the saddle. His horse shifted but stood obediently still under him.

"No. True. But He's the one who has the storm in His hand."

"He's got me there too. I can trust Him to look after me. He has so far."

"I don't think we're supposed to tempt Him. Jesus said something about that when Satan was trying to get him to throw himself off a cliff."

"I've never tried that anyway," Ryan said, his half grin showcasing the deep dimple in his cheek. With those twinkling blue eyes and the square jaw, Luke figured that it was no wonder the girls found him handsome.

Still, he was a bit of a wildcard, and Luke felt bad for any woman who tried to get him to settle down with her.

"There's a nasty rumor going around town that you're about to get hitched," Ryan said, sounding just as casual as he could be, but Luke understood now why he'd made the detour and stopped at the cottage.

"I guess it's not a nasty rumor if it's true." Luke didn't see any reason to deny it. "But I'm not sure she's decided to say yes or not."

"I didn't even know you were courting."

"Guess I wasn't."

"In fact, I didn't think you two got along at all."

"Maybe we would if I could avoid her grandma. That's my goal. See what I can work out with Kristin while avoiding Miss Heather like the plague."

"Seems to me like you got that backward." Ryan spoke, and Luke got the feeling that it was one of those rare moments where Ryan actually had a little bit of wisdom that maybe he should listen to.

"What do you mean?" he asked, after pondering it for just a moment.

"Miss Heather is on your side. If you want to get hitched up, and you don't know her that well, Miss Heather's the one that you need to have sweet on you."

It wasn't exactly what Ryan was saying, but Luke moved that around in his head. Maybe, maybe Ryan was right. Maybe he was thinking about it all wrong.

"So you think Miss Heather would convince Kristin that getting married to me is a good idea?"

"Maybe." Ryan shifted in the saddle while his horse swished his tail back and forth.

"So... What do you mean?"

"I mean, if you get married to Kristin, she lives with her grandma and those other two or three old ladies. Life's going to be pretty miserable if you don't get along with any of them."

"She can move out here." But even as Luke said that, he knew it was impossible. It was just a one-bedroom house. That was part of the reason why, when he had watched Becky to begin with, she hadn't stayed overnight at his house.

"Right." Ryan rolled his eyes. He knew as well as Luke what the cottage entailed. He helped Luke build it.

Luke chewed on his words for a bit.

Ryan said, "It's kinda like with a woman who has kids already. You want to win the kids over. You know? I mean, if the kids like you, that's going to go a long way toward getting a woman to like you. And if the woman already likes you, it's going to go a long way toward getting her to fall in love with you."

"You talk about this like you have experience." Luke was curious. He hadn't heard a thing about Ryan and any woman.

"Not me. I have friends. I've seen them go about it all wrong. They get in with the woman, and they kind of resent the kids. They're jealous and whatnot. To me, you just fight against yourself when you do that. You sweeten the kids up, and the woman kind of comes along. Plus, I haven't yet met a woman who could resist a man who's good with kids. Surely old ladies are about the same."

Luke wasn't quite sure that was true, but it had enough truth to it that he thought it might be a good idea for him to try it out.

"You sticking around for the winter?" he asked, figuring it was time to change the subject. He needed to think about what Ryan had said before he made any decisions. But he didn't need to keep talking to Ryan about it. It was his private life, and even though Ryan was his brother, he was unsettled enough that he didn't really want to talk about it. Not anymore.

"Maybe." Ryan looked over his shoulder. "The town hasn't changed any. And it's nice enough, I guess. It's quiet. And there ain't much to do. I mean, aside from work."

"That's true. I think that's part of its appeal for most people."

"Yeah. Maybe when I'm about fifty or so, I'll be ready to sit around and do nothing," he jerked his chin at Luke's boots which were propped up on the banister, "like you."

"I rolled up a hundred bales of hay this morning. Seems like I deserved a sandwich before I go gather them up and put them in the shed."

"You need a hand with that?"

"I'd appreciate it."

Ryan jerked his chin again. "I'll be back in fifteen."

He turned, allowed his horse to pick its way through the sand dunes, and then urged him into a canter as they hit the sand along the shore.

Luke figured he should have told him that if it started to rain, he'd wait and gather the bales in the morning. But maybe they could get a few in before the rain hit. In the meantime, he was looking forward to the rain, because he had a little courting to do.

Chapter 7

Kristin stood at the stove opening tea bags while the water heated for her to make sweet tea.

They'd had a little thunder and lightning, mostly wind, and now the rain was pouring down.

"Was that a knock?" Miss Alma said from where she sat with Miss Joyce and Kristin's gram at the kitchen table. They were knee-deep in a game of cards, and Kristin had gotten up in order to make everyone a little bit of refreshment.

"I think it's just the rain," Kristin said before the sound came again, and she thought that maybe Miss Alma was right, and it was a knock. "But I'll go check."

All three ladies had their heads up, like they were listening. It was an easy afternoon, with not much going on, which was typical for most of their afternoons unless someone had a doctor's appointment. Kristin found herself chauffeuring them back and forth to Blueberry Beach, usually at least once a week and sometimes more. Seemed like the older a person got, the more appointments they had.

Kristin didn't mind. The ladies were sweet, and she enjoyed their company. They were like their own little family, and it felt cozy and happy with everyone there.

She wiped her hands on a towel and hurried to the door. If it was someone out in the storm, even if they were standing under the porch, with the wind, they might be getting wet.

Their door didn't have a window or a keyhole, so she simply opened it up.

She almost slammed it right back shut, since Luke Landry stood there on the porch.

She hadn't seen him since they'd walked away from each other a week ago.

He said he was "willing" to marry her. Not eager, not excited, not anything. Just willing.

For some reason, she didn't jump on that. She figured if he was just willing, he could put out a little bit more effort to get back in touch with her.

Maybe, for Becky's sake, she should have put more effort into it. But she just couldn't. She'd do it, she was willing too, but she wasn't eager, either. Mostly because she wasn't sure she wanted to spend the rest of her life with someone who was just putting up with her. Willing.

Although, being willing made things a lot easier than being unwilling.

She could keep that in mind.

"Luke. I wasn't expecting you." She stated the obvious and then kicked herself for not sounding a little bit more intelligent. "You can come in."

"Actually, I'm here to see your gram."

"Oh." She supposed she thought he was there to talk to her about getting married and being parents to Becky. Silly her. Apparently. "Come on in. She's with her friends in the kitchen."

She stepped back, opening the door while he came in, his hat wet, dripping little beads of water. It looked clean, along with his jeans, and she loved those boots.

She hadn't thought she was a boot kind of girl, but seeing Luke in his boots did something to her heart.

It made it a little bit more than willing, she supposed.

As she closed the door, she said, "Did you need to talk to her by herself?" If he did, she could have Gram come out to the living room.

"Not really. Actually, I guess I could talk to all three of them. There are three, right?"

"Four. If you're talking about ladies that live with me. Miss Daisy just moved in, and it looks like she might be staying."

"Yes. I want to talk to all four of them."

"All right. Well... I was just making sweet tea, and if you don't mind, I can finish that, then I can let you guys have the kitchen." She wasn't sure what she had been thinking, but she didn't think that he was going to take her up on it. But he did, nodding his head as he took his hat off and held it in his hand.

"I'm still dripping. I can stand here for a bit, and that way you don't have to mop the floor after me."

"It's okay. Come on in. A little bit of rain never hurt anything."

She thought maybe his lips twitched, almost like they wanted to turn up in a friendly smile but he stopped them just in time.

She didn't know why she felt so uncomfortable, so defensive around him. He was a nice guy. Everyone liked him. They just...never got back on good footing after their near-death experience on the sailboat.

"Follow me," she said, leading the way to the kitchen. The house was huge, but it was laid out simply. With two large living rooms on either side of the front door, and a hall that led back to a large kitchen. There was a big dining room, a parlor, and someone through the years had added a sunroom.

She loved the old house. Loved it with every breath, and it was one of the reasons why she appreciated being able to take care of her gram and her three friends. She didn't have to have another job. The money that they paid her more than took care of her mortgage, the groceries, the various utility bills, with some left over that she called her salary every week.

"Ladies," she said as she walked into the kitchen, with three sets of old eyes looking at her. "I mentioned Luke a little a few times this week, and I think you all know him from church and around town, but in case you've never actually talked to him, this is Luke Landry."

They had more than one conversation about the craziness of her even considering getting married to someone she barely knew.

Actually, she was the only one who thought it was crazy. Gram wanted her to do it with every breath in her ninety-five-pound body. Miss Alma and Miss Joyce were on Gram's side as well, although Miss Joyce was more on the fence, because she believed that Kristin should marry someone who had money.

Miss Daisy, being new in town, hadn't been as vocal, but she'd been a silent partner on Team Luke. Except for the money issue.

It wasn't that Luke was dirt poor or anything, although she liked to think that it really wouldn't make a difference to her. She was happy where she was. Happy with what she was doing, and content with her life.

Maybe that was why she didn't want to upset the apple cart, and get a husband and child, possibly two children, and turn her nice, ordered world completely upside down.

But that reeked of selfishness. After all, a person only had one life, and they could either live it for themselves, or they could live it for the Lord. Seemed to her like if she were living it for the Lord, turning it upside down wouldn't be too much to ask.

"Luke Landry. So all of my helpful suggestions finally got through your thick head, and you saw my granddaughter for the jewel she is."

Luke seemed to be swallowing pretty hard, and Kristin wondered if maybe he was swallowing the words that wanted to come out and trying to think instead of words that should come out.

She tried not to giggle as she turned toward the stove, taking the pot of brewed tea and pouring it in the pitcher she'd filled with cold water and ice.

"Yes, ma'am. Guess you finally got through to me. I can't help it if I'm a bit of a lughead sometimes. Would you mind going out with me?"

Kristin almost dropped the pot.

She turned around, narrowing her eyes. Was this an alien impersonating Luke? Aliens did not belong in Strawberry Sands. Not even a little, but...it seemed very likely. More likely than Luke Landry agreeing with her gram. Calling himself a lughead, and... What had he just said?

"What?" She couldn't keep the word from escaping out of her mouth.

"I just asked your gram if she'd go out on a date with me. I...don't believe in dating more than one woman at a time, or I would ask these other lovely ladies if they'd like to come along."

He did. He said exactly what she thought she heard.

"I never believed in UFOs," she murmured as she turned back around.

She thought Luke snorted, but she couldn't be sure.

"You watch it, Missy. No wonder he doesn't want to take you out. It's that smart mouth of yours. UFOs. You just hold on to your hat while I run up and get myself ready, and we can go out on the town." Gram spoke as her chair scraped against the floor.

"Well, I was thinking about Friday night, but... I suppose right now is just fine."

"Life is short. Alma, Daisy, and Joyce might as well come with us. We can be like one of those shows on TV. You know, where the man has to choose between all the ladies which one he likes at the end of the evening."

"I see. Well—"

Kristin bit back a wicked, evil chuckle at Luke's inability to find his tongue.

He was no match for her gram. There weren't too many people who were. She felt bad for him and would have stepped in to rescue him, but she didn't know what to say. And he wasn't there to see her anyway.

If he was going to spend the evening with her gram, he was going to have to find his sea legs and figure out how to handle her.

Chapter 8

Luke had a hard time taking his eyes off Kristin. He didn't recall her hair ever being down like it was today. Usually, she had it up in a ponytail or braid or something, but today, it hung loose and was past her waist. It was distracting.

He couldn't remember what those tight pants things that his sisters wore sometimes too were called, but she had those on and a loose T-shirt over top of them.

Ever since she'd opened the door, he'd had trouble taking his eyes off her. Whether it was her sweet chocolate eyes or the rest of her that was so distracting, he couldn't quite tell.

Regardless, he'd been stumbling with his words ever since he walked in. If he didn't get himself gathered up, Miss Heather was going to make mincemeat out of him.

"I'm not sure how long you plan on being out, but I'm not as young as I used to be. I don't move quite as fast. It will take thirty minutes or an hour to get myself all dolled up and ready for a man as handsome as you. You might as well sit yourself down here at the table and have a glass of sweet tea." Miss Heather pointed at the chair she'd gotten out of. "Go ahead and talk to my granddaughter. She's a right nice girl. 'Course, she doesn't have as much experience as I do."

"I'm sure she doesn't," Luke said, smiling to himself. Ryan had been right. A little bit of buttering up had greatly improved the situation. Miss Heather wasn't trying to shove him into Kristin's face. She was too busy taking herself to the stairs, to get herself fixed up.

Of course, he hadn't planned on taking four ladies out this evening. He thought he would do it Friday night or Saturday. But there didn't seem to be any time like the present.

And before he knew it, the kitchen was empty, with the other ladies saying they needed to get dolled up as well and also let their other friend know her evening plans had changed, and he found himself watching the sway of Kristin's hair as she worked to make tea at the counter.

"That was slick," she said as the sound of thumping on the stairs faded.

"I didn't see a chairlift on the stairs."

"There isn't one. I've thought about that. I've also considered an elevator, but both of those things are rather pricey. The elevator being the most pricey."

"So it's money that's keeping you from putting that in?"

"Mostly," she said, turning around and carrying the tea to the table. "I guess I also feel like it'll ruin the look of the house. Not that that's more important than the well-being of my gram and the other ladies. But they don't quite need it yet, and I've been dragging my feet." She gave a little shrug, then turned back to the counter, getting in the cupboard and grabbing two glasses. "I'm sorry you're stuck with me. And from my experience with the ladies, it could be a while. Although all they're going to do is change their clothes and fix their hair."

"That's okay. I'm not in a rush. Although, I have to admit I was thinking I would ask her out on a date and we'd go, you know, on Friday."

"You have to be quick to get one up on my gram."

"I figured that out." He could hear the humor in his tone. It made Kristin smile, and he was struck again by how pretty she was. Maybe it was the sparkle in her eyes or the slight bit of pink to her cheeks. He wasn't entirely sure, but he did know that he had never noticed it before.

"I didn't really come to talk about what we talked about last week, but I've been thinking about it."

"Me too," she said, and her face held nothing but honesty and openness.

"It's my day to have Becky tomorrow. If... If you're considering everything that we suggested, you'd be welcome to spend the day with us."

She didn't say anything as she picked up a glass and poured tea into it. She touched the glass that sat closer to him. "Would you like some?"

He nodded. "Please."

She filled it up without saying anything, then set the tea down, her face thoughtful. She pulled a chair back and sat down.

"Part of me thinks I'm being selfish if I say no. And most of me wants to say let's just do it. But then I guess there's a part of me that says... Maybe it's my feminine vanity that rebels against the idea of spending my life with someone who's just putting up with me." She narrowed her eyes, thoughtfully, and looked at him. There wasn't any antagonism, and her words were said calmly and quietly. "Do you know what I mean?"

"I suppose." He hadn't really thought about it like that. He was more along the lines of he didn't want to go through with it and then have her back out if she decided she didn't want him. And that was after deciding whether or not he wanted to upend his life. "I think of a husband as a provider. I would be taking on responsibility for my wife and child, possibly two children, and...all the ladies that you have living with you too."

"They pay me," she offered.

"I guess I kind of figured they did. But they are your responsibility. If we were to get married, I would consider them mine as well."

She nodded. "I suppose it's a job, but I don't look at it that way. I do have enough left at the end of the month to consider myself a business owner, but... I just live frugally, and there isn't too much that I want or need."

"I guess that would be my responsibility too. I know that if it's God's will for us to provide a home and family for the little girls, all those things will fall into place, but I can't help thinking about them. You don't start building a building without counting the cost."

"And building a family takes a lot more than a building. A lot more years, a lot more energy and time, a lot more...everything."

"Exactly."

"It's a big cost."

"I agree." He touched his tea. "Do you think it's too expensive?"

"I don't think I've figured that out. Although, I feel like it should be."

"I agree."

He wanted to keep talking about that. Get it settled. Just say what they were going to do already. But with having sisters, he thought that maybe getting things settled wasn't as important as building a foundation. If she was going to say yes, they needed to have something to build on, and it needed to be solid. After all, they both just agreed that it was an expensive thing they were building. A priceless thing. A family.

"You seem content here in Strawberry Sands. Is that true?" He wanted to learn more about her, but he didn't know what to ask that wouldn't be too personal.

That seemed like a safe place to start.

"I love it here. I really love this house. And it's kind of crazy, and I hope you don't get overwhelmed tonight, but I love the ladies that live with me too."

"You're kind of like family here."

"Yeah. That's exactly it." Then she laughed. "You better consider that. If you decide to go through with this, you do realize you're going to be outnumbered seven to one."

It took a little bit to understand what she meant, and then he huffed out a laugh. "That's a good point. That's almost enough to make me jump up and go running out the door. I'm not sure I can handle being the only man in a house full of seven women."

"I hope you don't want to use the bathroom too often," she teased, and then she seemed to think she better set his mind at ease. "Most of the rooms have master baths. There are eight bedrooms, and only two of them have bathrooms they share."

"All right. Then chances are I'll be able to find someplace to use the restroom." He just thought of something. "I... I assumed if we went through with this, I'd be moving in here. My cottage along the lake only has one bedroom."

"Yeah. That makes the most sense."

She looked back down at her tea, and he thought maybe he was going to have to figure out something else to talk about. It seemed to be his job to keep the conversation going, or maybe it was just his job to help them get to know each other.

But before he thought of anything, she said, "What about you? Are you just here in Strawberry Sands because that's where your family is?"

"I'm sure that's a big part of it. I love them. Couldn't imagine living without them. But I love it here too. I guess I'll miss my cottage by the lake. It's cool to lie in bed and see the glow of the sunrise on the water. Or the glow of the moonlight on the waves. We're close here, but not so close that I'd be able to see it."

"Actually, from some of the upstairs bedrooms, you can. There are three that have views of the lake. Although, they're all occupied. I have one, Gram and Alma have the other two. I don't think you're going to get them to move." She smiled a little.

"I guess beggars can't be choosy," he said. "I'll be happy wherever."

They were kind of talking about it like they both already decided that the marriage was going to happen. The family, the kids. But neither one of them actually said that.

Although, he supposed from what they were saying they weren't going to share a room. He hadn't even really considered that. That would be something they would think about eventually, right?

Maybe they could talk about that some other time. Today didn't seem like the proper time. Especially since they hadn't even figured out if they were actually going to go through with it or not.

"We hurried just for you." Miss Heather waltzed into the kitchen. "Don't expect me to get ready this quickly every time we go out."

"You are assuming there's going to be a second date?" he said, rising from his chair with his eyes on the diminutive woman with the big personality. He had to say he admired her. She was tenacious, and she had grit as well as sass. He could see why Kristin was so fond of her.

"I've never dated someone who didn't. I can't imagine you're not like all the other men I know." Miss Heather grinned at him and waited.

Miss Alma and Miss Joyce and Miss Daisy were behind her, and he was suddenly overpowered with old lady perfume.

"I was just going to go to the diner, but you guys are so fancied up, we might have to head to Blueberry Beach."

"We don't want to be too hard on your pocketbook, and Griff is making his chicken alfredo bread boat this week anyway. I've had it once, and I wouldn't mind having it several more times. It's pretty doggone good." She glanced over at Kristin. "You should get the recipe from him."

"All right. If the diner's good for all of you, that's where we'll go."

"I'm sorry to leave you here by yourself, Kristin. Are you going to be okay?" Miss Heather said as she put a hand on Kristin's shoulder and seemed genuinely concerned that Kristin would be okay.

"I'm sure I will be just fine. I can find something to do. Maybe I'll take a bubble bath or something."

"This house is so big, you must spend hours cleaning it every week," Luke said, thinking that Kristin probably did a lot more work than anyone gave her credit for.

"There's a lot of cleaning," Kristin acknowledged. "And cooking, and I probably spend most of my time running to the doctors'." She smiled fondly at the ladies. "Not that I mind. I'm actually getting to be a bit of an expert at all things medical."

"I bet you are," he said, and he had to admit, he really didn't want to leave. He wanted to stay and talk to Kristin. Look at her. Be with her.

"I'm starving," Miss Heather said, slipping her hand through the crook of his elbow and tugging a little to get him started toward the door.

"Me too. Lunch was hours ago," Miss Alma said, grabbing his other arm.

He didn't have quite enough arms, but that seemed okay, since Miss Joyce and Miss Daisy didn't seem to mind clomping along behind him with their walkers.

"You guys can call me if you need me," Kristin said as they walked out of the kitchen.

"I'll have them back before midnight," Luke said, grinning at her a little, encouraged when she grinned back at him.

Maybe they needed to talk about the sailboat incident. Maybe they needed to talk about a lot of things, but he felt like tonight was a start, and he also felt like Ryan had had a good idea. Taking the ladies out had been brilliant.

Now, if he could only survive the evening.

Chapter 9

Kristin shoved her arms into her sweatshirt and pulled it over her head. She looked forward to her daily morning walks, since it was often the only time during the day she had a quiet moment or two.

She loved her grandma and her friends, but they could be rather demanding.

Opening the door of the big old house quietly, she slipped outside.

Taking a deep breath of the lake-fresh air, she walked across the porch, down the steps, and started down the sidewalk toward the lake. There wasn't anything better than a morning walk along the beach, with the sunrise glistening off the waves and horses grazing contentedly on the hill.

Sometimes she saw Luke out feeding the horses on her morning walks.

She certainly didn't take the walks in order to see him, but in the last week or so, she found herself looking for him.

Actually, if she were being honest, she'd looked for him before that.

Maybe there was a reason why her gram had narrowed her sights on Luke as the person that she most badgered to get married to her granddaughter.

Kristin tried hard to not allow herself to have any kind of special favoritism toward him, but her gram was astute and probably had things figured out.

What things, Kristin wasn't sure.

Just as she wasn't exactly sure how the evening had gone the night before.

They were all laughing when they came in, but Luke hadn't stayed. He thanked the ladies for a good evening, bid Kristin a good night, shoved his hat back on his head, and left.

As happy as the ladies were, they were also exhausted, and all four of them went directly to bed. They might have been giddy as schoolgirls, but they certainly didn't have schoolgirl energy.

Not for the first time, Kristin wished she had dogs to walk. One of the ladies had brought one with her, but it had passed away not long ago. Miss Alma had been watching two for her granddaughter, but her granddaughter had come and taken them home. At the time, Kristin figured that her hands were already full enough, she probably didn't need to add a dog to the mix, as much as she wanted one.

Just something to take with her in the mornings, something that wouldn't break into her solitude but would allow her to have a little bit of companionship.

As she turned along the beach, she waved to Kim and Davis Thatcher, who were sitting out on their deck, coffee mugs on the table steaming in front of them.

The baby they shared wasn't anywhere in sight, and Kristin assumed she was still sleeping.

Early mornings weren't known as being romantic, but Kristin could see the benefits of a married couple getting up early and spending some quality time together.

Maybe they were reading the Bible and doing devotions together. That gave Kristin a small thread of longing which pulled like a string tightening around her chest.

She wouldn't mind having that. A husband to wake up with, to pray with, to read the Bible with, to discuss things that mattered to both of them with.

She tried to push those thoughts aside. She didn't want to be discontent with her life. It was a good life, a happy life, and she was content.

Of course, if she went through with the marriage, her entire life was going to be capsized.

She might as well enjoy what she had while she had it, because now more than ever, she understood that life could change at any moment.

If she had two young girls living at home, would she still be able to take her morning walks?

She'd been looking out at the lake as she walked, but movement caught her eye, and she turned her head toward the horse pastures, first seeing several horses with their heads up, galloping along the top of the rise, the orange glow of the sunrise adding drama to their silhouette. Drama and beauty.

Then she realized a man walked along the bottom of the fence coming in her direction.

It didn't take her long to recognize Luke. He wore jeans and boots and a sweatshirt as well as his cowboy hat.

But he didn't seem to be paying attention to the horses. In fact, it almost seemed like he was focused on her.

She slowed.

"Kristin! I was hoping to see you this morning. Do you have a minute?" Luke called as he got a little closer.

She stopped. Funny that her heart was doing all kinds of crazy things in her chest.

"Sure," she said, surprised at how calm she sounded.

"Want to walk on the beach?"

"You do that in your cowboy boots?"

He laughed. "I've been walking in the sand in my cowboy boots all my life. I'm actually pretty good at it if I do say so myself."

"All right." She smiled. She'd left her flip-flops back at the dunes when she crossed them to get to the beach.

It was a little cold on her feet, but like Luke, she'd been walking in her bare feet on the beach all of her life. Her feet had mostly gotten used to it. Although every winter they got soft, and every spring she had to harden them up a little.

"I had a good time with your gram and her friends last night. Did you talk to them?" he started as they moved along the shore, the waves lapping the sand.

"You must have tuckered them out, because I barely got any words out of them at all before they walked upstairs and went to bed. I really heard nothing about what happened. Although, I'm guessing that will be the talk of the morning this morning."

"They're not up yet?"

"Gram might be, I think sometimes she sits in bed and reads her Bible and just takes a little while to get up. After all, there's nothing that demands our attention every day, so there's no need to rush to get out of bed."

"What are you gonna do when she can't?"

She thought of that often over the last year or so that her grandma had been living with her. What was she going to do?

"I guess I'll just take it a day at a time. There's no point in worrying about something that might never happen."

"I think that's a good idea." He wasn't patronizing her; he actually sounded like he agreed with her that there was no point in borrowing trouble.

"I guess if I thought about it, I would be worried, but I don't mean to be putting you off or anything."

"No. I agree. You know, it's funny all the things we worry about that never happen. But we've wasted our time, made ourselves sick over it, and then something else happens that totally negates whatever it was we were concerned about."

"Right. But I suppose that's something that you might want to think about. After all, if we do what we're thinking about doing…" She didn't mean to bring the subject up. She wasn't going to if he didn't, but now that she had, she continued on. "It'll be something that you have to think about. And I honestly don't know. I didn't promise her that I wouldn't take her to a nursing home or anything."

"Would you?"

She wasn't sure if he was asking if she would promise, or if she would take her to a nursing home.

"I guess all the options are open. I… I do feel like it's a family's responsibility to take care of their parents. Just families are supposed to look out for each other. That's what families are for."

"That's not something that everyone believes."

"I think it's probably something that most people don't believe. Or maybe we just believe that we're supposed to pay for someone else to take care of them. And I can't blame people for wanting to do that. It's a hard job."

"You make it look easy."

He had been watching her? Or was he just saying that? Luke didn't seem like the kind of person who just said things, so maybe he truly had been paying attention.

"Thank you. I think."

"It was a compliment. Truly. You always seem happy. And last night as I was eating, I mean, don't get me wrong, the ladies are lovely and I love them, but I wasn't unhappy when it was time to go home. And I thought that you typically don't get to go home. That was your life."

"Maybe that's why I love my morning walk so much. It's just my time to be alone. No one's complaining, no one's arguing or fussing at me, or telling me how I need to go out and get a man. Or sometimes they tell me how I don't need to go out and get a man. It's kind of funny when you think about it."

"I'm glad you can laugh. I know I've gotten annoyed at times, and you paid the price for that. And I'm sorry."

"Not your fault. My gram can try a saint's patience."

"You must be a saint."

She shook her head, but she didn't say anything more. She thought maybe he was flattering her, and she didn't like it. She wanted sincere compliments or nothing. But maybe she was judging too harshly. Maybe he really was sincere. She just didn't see herself that way. Didn't see herself as anything out of the ordinary.

"Believe it or not, I wasn't really thinking that I would talk about your gram or her friends this morning."

"So you planned on meeting me?" she asked with surprise in her voice. She had thought this was a chance meeting.

"I happened to notice that you walk along the beach in the mornings. You've done it for years."

"I have." There was something about his words that made her glow inside. He had noticed her. For years. She supposed that wasn't that big of a deal. After all, his farm bordered the beach where she walked every morning. It made sense that he would see her. She'd seen him. She knew he fed his horses in the morning. She knew approximately what time he was out. It wasn't news.

But if she were being perfectly honest, Luke's brothers also lived on the farm and worked on it, and she had no idea what their schedules were. She saw them around but didn't pay attention to the hours they kept.

That was very telling.

"I just wanted to make sure that it would be okay that you and I spend the day with Becky. And I was hoping that we could pick up her sister too. I think her name is Rita?"

"Yeah. Rita, and she lives just outside of Strawberry Sands, on the right. The house is a little...run down."

"The one with the fenced yard?"

"Yes." The yard was fenced, but the fence was very dilapidated, and the front yard looked more like a junkyard than a nice place for kids to play.

"Would you like me to try to pick her up by myself? Or should we go together? Or you do it?" He laughed. "I think that would be all the options."

She laughed along with him. "I'll go with you. Or whatever. I guess I don't have a huge preference. Although, maybe I don't want to go by myself. It...doesn't always feel very safe there." She felt like a baby, because a child lived there. So it should be safe. It just didn't feel like the kind of place where a person went unless they had someone to watch their back.

"All right. Normally when I have Becky, she stays at my mom's house, and I go have breakfast with her. Do you think we should try to pick up her sister before or after we eat breakfast with Becky?"

"It might be a nice surprise for Becky if we have her there for breakfast. What do you think?"

"Sounds good. I'm pretty sure my mom has their phone number. She got it from Becky the last time she was there. I'll call and see if I can set something up."

"All right."

They walked a few more paces before he shoved his hands in his pockets and hunched his shoulders against a sudden big gust of wind. "You know, part of me is excited about this, and part of me is scared to death. But the idea of picking up Becky's sister and having Becky for the day along with you makes this all feel real, you know?"

"I know what you mean. It's like a trial for the real thing."

"Is there going to be a real thing?" he asked, and his voice sounded a little uncertain, like he hadn't made the decision, and he was asking her to make it for him.

"I don't know. What do you think?" she asked, truly unsure.

"The human part of me is scared to death. I've already said that. But the spiritual part of me? The part where I prayed about it? I feel like it's a big green light. It couldn't be any more obvious to me that God wants this to happen."

"That's pretty much the way I feel too. That this is what I'm supposed to do, even if it's not exactly what I want to do."

"Is the idea of being married to me that terrible?" His voice was studiously casual, and she wondered if maybe he was as sensitive to that as what she was when he had said he was "willing."

"No. It has nothing to do with marrying you. Actually, if it were just marrying you, I think I would be...maybe not eager, but much less apprehensive. Which is kind of funny, because if we were getting married, we would probably eventually have children, and that's exactly what we're going to be having if we go ahead with what we're doing. It just...wouldn't be sprung on us the way it will be."

He laughed, like he understood her rambling. She hadn't really meant to talk about them having children; that was a little bit awkward. After all, she wasn't even entirely sure that they should even get married, let alone get married and have kids. But he didn't have a reaction, and it made her more at ease.

"I think it's one thing to have children that are born one at a time and raised up in your house. It's another thing to have them come in, and you're really not even sure of where they're at. As much as I love Becky, there's so much about her that we don't know. And she doesn't really know us. For that matter, we don't know each other."

She understood what he was saying. They didn't know each other any more than they knew the children. And yet they were going to try to put everything together and throw it in a big house and make a family out of it. It seemed kind of fanciful.

"I would almost say that it's impossible to have that happen, except...God."

"I wouldn't even be considering it if I didn't think it was what the Lord wanted. But because I'm pretty sure that's what God wants me to do, I feel confident going ahead. The problem is, sometimes God wants us to do things just so they will fail, and we'll learn those lessons." He paused, reaching a hand out of his pocket and putting it down on his head like he didn't want his hat to blow away. "I don't like to fail."

"Me either. And I guess failure really isn't an option for me with this."

"I suppose it depends on what your definition of failure is."

"That's a good point. I guess...divorce. To me, divorce is failure."

"I don't like to even think that word, let alone say it out loud."

"Me either. That is the opposite of everything that I want. I mean, the kids, Becky and Rita, I want to do everything in my power to make sure that they have everything they need to grow up to be successful adults, including as much love as I can give them. But that's not really something I can control, you know? So much of it is going to be them making the right decisions."

"Where we don't have control. We can get them on the school bus in the morning, but we can't make them stay awake for their classes during the day, or pay attention, or make the right friends, or make the right decisions at all."

"Exactly. But with our marriage, that's us." She slowed, and he slowed beside her, then she stopped. "This is usually as far as I go."

"You need to get back. I'm sorry. I was so deep in thought that I didn't even realize how far we'd walked."

"Your cottage is up there somewhere, isn't it?" she asked, nodding toward the beach that stretched off in the distance.

"It is." He grinned a little. "Maybe we can go see it when we have the girls. Although, it's really nothing much. Just a kitchen, dining room, and living room all together and then one bedroom. It's pretty small, but big enough for me."

"Especially since you're not in it much anyway. Seems like you're either working on the farm or helping your mom at the bed-and-breakfast."

It was his turn to look at her, and she wished she wouldn't have said anything. Obviously she knew a little more about him than passing casual interest.

But he let it slide, and she appreciated it. She didn't want to explain why she knew so much about him.

She wasn't sure she could explain it to herself, other than she'd always been interested. Just interest, nothing more.

At least that's what she told herself, but she wasn't entirely sure it was true.

<h1 style="text-align:center">Chapter 10</h1>

Luke and Kristin turned around and started walking back down the beach.

"I can see why you do this every morning. It's pretty relaxing," he said, and she got the idea that he just wanted to have a casual conversation with her. Most of their conversations had involved things that they had to do, that they had to hash out, like getting the girls and discussing whether or not they should get married.

They were hardly typical conversations a couple might have in any sense of the word.

"I guess it's relaxing the same way it would be relaxing to come out and work with your horses every morning, being able to see this view. And do what you love, in one of the best places on earth."

"We're not biased." He laughed, and she laughed along with him.

"I can't think of anywhere else I'd rather live."

"You know, me either. I thought about moving away a few times. Back when I was younger," he added quickly, when her head turned at his statement. "I'm not even sure why. I guess sometimes you just feel pressure to do things. You know, be successful in the eyes of the world or whatever. But God gave me such a beautiful place. He gave me a family and a town, and it just seems silly to think that there was somewhere else that would be better. Maybe I could make more money, but money can't buy a life like this." He looked out toward the lake and then looked around the rolling hills with the horses grazing and the big sky overhead, that was now fully blue with the sun slowly moving up from the eastern horizon.

"You know, I wanted to apologize about the sailboat thing for a really long time." His words were said softer, and with a lot of hesitancy, like he wasn't sure how she was going to take them.

"I should apologize too. I know it takes two to fight."

She'd forgotten some of the details of that day. Like how they both ended up on the dock where several people who were renting the bed-and-breakfast for the summer had kept their boats.

The dock had long since rotted and been swept away by the lake, but back then, it was typical to have ten or so boats docked there every summer.

Neither one of them had ever done much boating, but they'd watched more than once as boaters had gotten their crafts ready and taken them out on the lake.

However they'd ended up on the dock, they had been arguing about whether or not they could man a sailboat.

"I can't even remember what it was that you said that made me so mad."

"I can't remember either, but I do remember that I was deliberately baiting you. You got so angry, and it was… Somehow it made me feel good to make you angry. That's sick, I know, but maybe that's just the way teen boys are."

"It might be. But whatever it was, I remember later thinking that it was stupid for me to get mad. I knew that you were just saying things to try to upset me. I played right into your hands."

"You did. I really wanted to get on the sailboat, and you practically forced me to get on, once you were so upset with me that you had to prove that I was wrong."

"Have you gotten so angry that all you see is just red? Like a red haze just descends over your vision?"

"Once or twice, and pretty much always with you involved."

She laughed. She knew he didn't mean anything by it. He was just being honest. "That's what I saw that day. Just red. I wasn't thinking with my brain, I was thinking with my emotions, and all I wanted was to prove you wrong."

"I think we both proved ourselves wrong," he said after a bit.

They had managed to get the sailboat away from the dock, and they got the sails unfurled too. But neither one of them knew how to run it, and they ended up out in the middle of the lake before they knew what hit them.

"It's amazing that we didn't capsize the boat." She had thought that over and over again.

"And neither one of us were wearing life vests. That was the stupidest thing I've ever done. I was scared to death, because I knew that if anything were to happen to the boat and we ended up in the lake, both of us were going to die. I didn't want to die," he said softly. "And I definitely didn't want you to die."

"I kinda thought you did. That day anyway. And for a long time, I hugged the idea that you were trying to kill me close. But in my rational mind, I knew that you weren't so desperate to kill me that you would die yourself."

"Yeah. I definitely didn't want to kill you. I... I kinda liked you."

She laughed. "You have an interesting way of showing it."

"I think that's a junior high boy for you."

"I could really get into the idea of segregated schools. Segregated by sex. It seems like the stupidity of junior high boys is only matched by the stupidity of junior high girls."

Their laughter rang out, and Kristin realized that far from being upset about the subject matter, she was enjoying their conversation. It was...funny almost. Even though she'd been scared to death, more scared than she'd ever been in her life before or after. Now, they were laughing about it. And she wasn't bothered at all.

"I didn't think I would ever forgive you for what you did. And now, it just seems like one of those things."

"It ended well. We were saved, the boat was saved, and that's really all that matters in the end, I suppose."

"Well, both of us spent a long time paying for it. I was scared to death I was going to go to jail. Dr. Branson must have been laughing the whole time, but he looked as scary as he could possibly be when he told us that the only way he was going to not have the police come and arrest us and take us to jail was if we agreed to pay him three thousand dollars each. I worked three summers in order to earn that much."

"My family really suffered because of that fine," he said low. "I think I blamed you for that more than anything. Even though it was obviously not your fault. No more than it was mine alone. Because you didn't hold a gun to my head and make me get on that boat. I goaded you into it."

"I feel like I should apologize to your mom. It never occurred to me that your family suffered."

"Yeah."

"Those were the last three summers I had with my aunt. I ended up working my butt off, and I guess I blamed you for the fact that she passed away and I never really got to spend any more days on the beach with her. It... Instead of taking responsibility for my own actions, it was just nicer to blame you."

"We were a pair. That's for sure. At least, at this point in my life, I can realize that I was one hundred percent to blame. And I'm sorry that I allowed it to color my interactions with you from there on out."

"I'm sorry too." She looked over at him, hoping he could see the sincerity on her face. She meant every word of it. She didn't mean to ruin her relationship with Luke for the rest of her life over something so dumb. But that's what she had done. Rather than taking responsibility for it herself, she blamed him, and the payment had been a lack of a relationship.

"Kristin?" Luke said, and she loved the way her name rolled off his tongue. It sent something warm and good down her back.

She thought about that, and she almost didn't answer him.

"Yeah?" she finally said, feeling like she had to pull herself out of a trance.

"I guess I still like you. Despite all the animosity that lay between us. Maybe that's part of the reason that the idea of an improvised marriage to you didn't feel like such a bad idea to me."

"I've always admired you," she said immediately. That was so true. She had. "And I've always been interested in you. Wanting to know what you're doing, where you are, and watching you. So yeah. I guess the animosity was there, but I think the reason that Gram zeroed in on you was because she could tell that there's never been anyone as interesting to me as you."

That was far more than she intended to say.

"I think we can make this work," he said in that same low tone.

"I think we will. Both of us are headstrong and stubborn, and we just need to get headstrong and stubborn about the right things. You know?"

"Staying married. We'll be stubborn about that. And we'll be stubborn about raising these girls to the best of our ability."

"That's exactly right. We'll just use our bad qualities for good."

He laughed. "I'm not sure I've ever had anyone present it to me quite like that, but you've got a point. Stubbornness isn't exactly an endearing quality, but it can be a good thing. As long as we make sure that we use it the right way."

"And we will," she said, lifting her chin and looking him in the eye, feeling more than ever that this was something that was going to work out exactly the way they wanted it to.

"So…" He paused, and she realized that they had stopped and were facing each other. "Should we set a date?" He lifted his brows, as though he was asking her, like the decision was hers.

"I think we should. I mean, we're going to be spending the day with the girls, and that will give us an idea, but we're not going to let anything that happens today make us change our minds, right?"

"Even if the girls fight the entire day, set the house on fire, and pull a knife on us?"

"You really know how to do worst-case scenarios, don't you?"

He laughed. "I had siblings."

"I didn't. And I always wanted them. Maybe that's why it tugs at my heart so hard that Becky wants to be with her sister. I wanted a sibling so bad. Everybody else had one. I felt like it would be a built-in playmate."

"A built-in fighting partner sometimes too. I know my mom complained that some days it felt like all us kids did was fight with each other. And I remember a lot of fighting. But I also remember a lot of good times where we got along too."

"Those are beautiful memories. I suppose you should appreciate them."

"And we can make sure that Becky and Rita have those memories."

"That's right." She wanted to ask about other children. Would there be more? But… She wasn't sure she was ready to have that conversation yet. Maybe he wasn't ready either. After all, they were taking some really big steps.

"So you asked about a day. I can do pretty much any time. I know next week there aren't any doctor's appointments, and that's usually what I have to work my schedule around."

"All right. Then…we're going to do this fast?"

"Let's not waste any time."

"I guess that's how I feel about it. Let's get married, we'll get Becky settled in with us, and then we'll work on getting Rita."

"That sounds like a plan." Her stomach was churning, because up until this point, it had been vague ideas, but now that he laid it out, it felt like it was concrete and not just something that they were talking about.

"Are you thinking about backing out?"

"No. I'm nervous and scared to death, but no. I'm not backing out." She could live scared. She could live nervous too, but she didn't have to do either.

There was nothing to be afraid about if she was doing God's will. Everything might not work out, but everything would be what God wanted it to be. Of that, she was sure.

Chapter 11

About an hour after he left Kristin, Luke's phone rang.

He smiled when he saw that it was Kristin. And then he realized she probably wouldn't be calling him if something wasn't seriously wrong. They were supposed to go pick up Rita. In fact, he had been planning on leaving in fifteen minutes to pick Kristin up to go get her.

Becky had stayed the night at his mother's house, and he had arranged to pick Rita up. Her foster parents had not been the most pleasant people to work with, but they had seemed eager to get rid of Rita for the day.

Tamping down the uneasy thoughts he had, telling himself he was borrowing trouble, he answered his phone.

"Hello?"

"Luke. I'm so sorry to bother you."

"Not a bother," he said quickly.

"All right. I just got a call from the doctor's office. Gram had an appointment last week, and she had some blood work done. Apparently some of it came back with some bad numbers. They want to see her in the office first thing this morning."

"Wow. If they called this early, it must be pretty serious."

"You know how doctors are. They wouldn't give me much information over the phone. So I don't know, but that's what I thought too."

"All right. I'll pick Rita up by myself. She, Becky, and I will hang out until you're back. We'll wait to take a ride until then. Can you come to my cottage?"

"Sure. If you want to hang out at my house with the ladies, you can do that too. They talked about making bread with the girls the next time they came."

He tried to decide whether he wanted homemade bread bad enough to do the work that it would take to get it.

"All right. Then I'll get Rita, and we'll eat at my mom's, then we'll go to your house. That's where we'll be whenever you get back."

"Assuming I get back. I'm... I'm not sure what they're going to have us do."

He could hear the worry in her voice. He wanted to do something to ease it. But he didn't have any words of comfort or assurance that she didn't already know.

"Whatever happens, I'll be here with you. And we already know God's got this."

"You're right. I don't know why I'm worried. I guess... I guess it's just the idea that the doctor calls and there's something wrong and you know your life is going to change. I hate change."

"There's been a lot of changes in your life. That's for sure."

"Some of them I'm looking forward to," she said, and he wondered which ones exactly that they were. It almost seemed like she might be saying that she was looking forward to being with him. Could that be it?

He didn't want to give himself too much credit. And he didn't want to get his hopes up either. He also didn't want to take time to ask her, especially since she had other things she probably needed to do.

"Is there anything you need me to take care of?" he asked.

"No. I think the ladies will be fine. I just try to keep an eye on them. Every once in a while, they use the stove or the oven and forget to turn it off. I do that too, so I don't think it's necessarily age-related. As much as...just not always paying attention."

"All right. I'll make sure they don't burn the house down. I kind of figured that already, but thanks for the reminder."

She laughed, which was his intention.

"Kristin?"

"Yeah?"

"Thanks for calling." He had to admit, it was nice to hear from her.

"Thanks for answering. Thanks for the laugh. I needed it. I'm feeling a lot better. Like I can face whatever this is going to be."

"And you won't be doing it alone," he reminded her.

"You're right."

Whether she knew that he was talking about him being with her, or whether she was thinking that the Lord was with her, they were both true thoughts. They hung up, and he realized that now he was going to have to go face Rita's foster parents himself.

It wasn't going to be that bad, he told himself as he finished up feeding hay to the horses that were in the paddock area before he got in his pickup and headed toward the other side of town.

"It is not going to be that bad," he reminded himself as he looked at the old car parts and bare dirt in the front yard of the foster parents' house.

The Cliffords. He was pretty sure that was their name.

A dog, some kind of muddy brown color, with a three-inch-thick collar with spikes that stuck out of it, barked from the other side of the fence. It looked like a golden retriever that might have been mixed with Rottweiler, not that Luke was any expert on dogs.

He'd had one growing up, but it had died several years ago. He just hadn't gotten another one. He wasn't sure why.

Even though this dog looked a little ferocious, there was something about it, maybe the muddy brown fur or the sad eyes that looked more hungry than angry.

Whatever it was, he didn't allow the barking to bother him but opened the gate and strode into the yard.

The dog quit barking as soon as it could walk over and sniff him. He stopped and put a hand out so the dog could sniff it. Once it had, he patted it on the head and said, "Good boy."

The dog's tail wagged, and it whined a bit.

So much for being a great watchdog. He chuckled a little. Golden retrievers were known for their friendly personalities, and sometimes he thought the Rottweilers' reputations weren't deserved. Whatever it was, the dog was just as friendly as he thought it would be. And he found himself wishing that he could take Rita *and* the dog for the day. Or keep them both forever.

"I'm sorry, buddy. I only have permission for the girl."

The dog whined like it understood what he was saying and then stuck its tongue out and licked the palm of his hand as he patted its head.

"Good boy," he said as he started toward the door.

He knocked but didn't hear a sound from inside the house.

It didn't seem like anyone was up. Then, he saw movement at the window, like the curtain was being pulled back. Two little eyes stared up at him before the curtain fell back.

There were several moments of pause, and he thought that maybe whoever it was looking at him had run in the opposite direction. Maybe no one was going to let him in. He had his hand raised to knock again when the door opened, and a scruffy little girl, her blonde hair in tangles around her face, and smudges of dirt on her cheeks and arms, stood in her bare feet, with a nightgown that didn't quite make it to her knees. It looked like she'd worn it for several days and nights, as cruddy as it was.

"Mr. Luke?" the little girl said, seeming equal parts shy and outgoing. Like she couldn't quite decide whether she wanted to be friendly or wanted to be cautious.

"That's right. I'm supposed to be here to pick up a Miss Rita Peck."

"That's me," the little girl said, her chest sticking out just a bit more, her lips lifting up at the use of her full name with a Miss in front of it.

He wasn't as charming as some of his brothers, but it looked like he had been able to charm Rita. He liked that. And he immediately liked the little girl too. She opened the door wider and then said, "You better stand out here. Josie Mae and Bubba aren't up yet. And... I might get in trouble if I let you in. They told me I'm not allowed to let strangers inside ever. Even though you're not a stranger, I still don't want to get in trouble."

"And I don't want you to get in trouble. I'll stand here. What's the dog's name?"

"That's Bruno. And he really likes his belly rubbed. Bubba says he's a pain and a terrible watchdog, but he's my friend."

"I see."

"And he doesn't bark at my sister when she visits me, and that's the best thing. Because Bubba and Josie Mae don't like it when she comes."

"They don't like it when your sister visits?" Luke asked, hardly daring to believe that Rita's foster parents wouldn't encourage her to have a relationship with her sister.

"No. They don't like me to have friends over. At all."

"Why not?" Luke asked, not liking the direction this conversation had taken.

Rita shrugged a thin little shoulder, and the look on her face said she had no idea.

She was just a kid. She probably really didn't know.

Maybe they were hiding something. Maybe they were just antisocial. Or maybe they were afraid that Rita would be badly influenced by people. Although, Luke was hardly thinking that was the case.

"Well, Bruno and me will sit out here and wait as long as it takes. There's no rush." He looked down at Bruno, who, with his sad, droopy eyes, looked a little ridiculous with the tough boy collar, with the spikes sticking out.

Luke was tempted to take the collar off, but he didn't want to rock any boats.

Instead, he turned around, walked to the step, slid down a little bit so he wasn't right by the rotten board, and sat down.

As anticipated, Bruno followed him, whining. Luke suspected he was hungry and wished he had brought something to feed him. But he hadn't anticipated meeting a hungry dog on the way to pick up Becky's little sister.

The little girl had disappeared from the door, but she hadn't closed it. Bruno ignored the open door and instead stood by Luke who scratched him between the ears. When he stopped, Bruno pushed his nose into his shoulder to remind him that he was still standing there, and he still wanted to be petted.

Eventually, Bruno ended up on the floor with all four paws in the air while Luke scratched his belly.

The dog felt dirty, mangy even, and Luke saw several fleas skittering around in his fur.

It made him itchy, but he didn't move. The dog was enjoying his scratching way too much.

An idea started to come to him as he sat there with the dog.

"They said I can go," Rita said as she appeared back in the doorway, still dressed in her dingy nightgown with her hair in a mess. She hadn't touched water between the last time he'd seen her and now.

"Awesome. Do you need to take anything with you?" he asked.

She shook her head.

"Do you think we could take Bruno?"

Her eyes lit up. "Would you?" she asked, looking more excited than she had since she arrived.

He nodded. "If it's okay with your parents, we'll take him too."

"I'll go ask." She started to run away, but then she turned around. "And they're not my parents."

He jerked his head up, acknowledging her words. He hadn't meant to make such an obvious mistake; she had been using their names, not calling them mom and dad. So it was obvious she hadn't considered them her parents. He wasn't well-versed in foster children and didn't know whether they typically called the people they were living with by their first names or not.

This time when the little girl returned, there was a man in a dirty white T-shirt and baggy basketball shorts along with her. He looked like he'd just woken up, with sleep lines along the side of his face, his eyes bloodshot.

"You want to take that mangy dog with you?" the dude said, with no greeting or introduction.

"I do. Actually, I have a hundred bucks in my pocket, and I'll give it to you."

He wasn't sure where that came from. He'd just stuck the money in his pocket that morning. Someone had come and bought a big round bale of hay. And had paid with a hundred-dollar bill.

He hadn't intended to spend it and certainly not on a dog that wasn't worth a tenth of that much.

"You'd give me a hundred dollars for the dog?" the man said, disbelief making his voice squeaky.

"Said I would."

"Lots of people say stuff. Let me see the money." The man jerked his head, like he didn't believe that Luke actually had a hundred bucks.

Kind of funny that the man had completely forgotten about the girl that he was supposed to be concerned about and was more interested in the dog. He hadn't even come to the door for the girl.

Luke reached in his pocket and pulled out the hundred-dollar bill.

"That fake?" the man said, squinting his eyes at the bill like he was going to be able to tell whether it was hot off the presses or not.

"I don't think so. Somebody bought hay off me this morning. This is what they paid me with. I'll give it to you, and I'll take your dog and have Rita for the day."

"I never heard anybody so dumb, wants to give me a hundred bucks for a mangy old dog what ain't worth nothing. But some folks ain't got no sense." He jerked his head again and scratched in the general area below his waist. Luke averted his eyes.

"You want it?" Luke asked, holding up the bill.

"Take the dog. He's a worthless piece of crap." He started to turn away, then stopped. "Have the girl back before I go to bed tonight. I don't want her waking me up when she comes in."

"Yes, sir," Luke said. Although there were other words he wanted to say, he bit them back.

He handed the hundred-dollar bill over to the man, a little bit sad, because even though he might have helped Bruno, the man was probably just going to get a different dog to replace him.

A different dog that would have the exact same life, but Luke had done what he could here, and Rita was his main concern. This was no place for a little girl. If he had any doubts about whether or not he was doing the right thing, they had disappeared at what he had seen that morning.

He couldn't wait to tell Kristin what he had seen.

His doubts evaporated even more as he watched Rita hug her sister Becky at his mom's house. That was after he dropped Bruno off at his sister's dog salon, explaining that the dog had fleas and who knew what else. She assured him that she would give him the best treatment she could and would call him when the dog was ready.

"Are you excited about baking bread today?" he asked the girls as they sat at the table shoveling pancakes into their mouths like they hadn't eaten in a week. They nodded their heads while chewing big mouthfuls.

They'd helped his mom mix them up and cook the first few.

Then, she'd made them all sit down at the table so they could eat while she finished cooking the rest.

Luke had found that his appetite had fled. There weren't too many times in his life where he hadn't been able to eat, but today was one of them. It was urgent that he and Kristin get married as soon as possible and get started trying to get those girls together in their home. Becky needed a home, and Rita needed out of the one that she was in. He was sure of that with his entire being.

He didn't stay long at his mom's house but waved goodbye, thanking her for the breakfast. And promising that he would bring her the groceries she'd ordered from the grocery store the next day.

He seldom paid his mom for the things he ate at her house, but he tried to do as many odds-and-ends jobs as he could for her.

Gathering the girls up, they walked catty-corner across the street to Kristin's house. He hoped she wouldn't be long. He had a lot of things he needed to talk to her about.

Chapter 12

Lena cleaned up the dishes, humming softly to herself.

If she had extra clothes in her house, she would have offered Rita something to wear. As it was, she had put a bug in Luke's ear that maybe he ought to get her some clothes. The poor thing shouldn't be walking around in a see-through nightgown the way she was. Lena was pretty sure the little girl wasn't wearing underwear.

She figured that this would be good for her son, although he was definitely out of his element. But it had gotten Kristin and Luke together, when Lena hadn't been sure that anything actually would, even though those two belonged together, and the entire town knew it.

Miss Heather knew it too, but her way of going about getting them together had ended up having the opposite effect. Which was too bad, because Miss Heather was a nice lady.

Lena continued to hum to herself as she finished cleaning up the kitchen. She loved it when her kids visited. And she loved seeing them settle into their lives, doing good in the world.

Taking one last look around the kitchen, seeing that it was spick-and-span in case any late-coming guests walked through it, she grabbed a windbreaker, slipped her flip-flops on, and headed for the door.

She'd been checking on the old fellow who lived in the lighthouse more and more. He seemed to be getting more frail. She found out his name was Joe, and he allowed her to give him what she claimed were leftovers. She didn't tell him that she made the things just for him.

Grabbing the casserole that she'd set on the stand right by the door so she wouldn't forget it, she let herself out of the house and started walking toward the beach.

Joe had been giving her all his chocolate-covered espresso beans, the ones he got from his son in the city.

Lena couldn't help herself from being a little upset at the son. It seemed like the man needed to come back and give his dad a hand. But a man like Joe was hard to do things for. He had a lot of pride, and he probably didn't want to bother his son, make him lose work, or give up his life in the city completely to take care of him. And Joe would never leave his lighthouse.

Lena had talked to him enough to know that Joe had lived there all his life, he and his wife had raised their three children there, even though it had been rather cramped.

Now that ships didn't need lighthouses anymore, Joe had retired, but he still lived frugally in his beloved lighthouse.

It was a bit of a walk up the beach, and her arms were tired by the time Joe came into view.

He was already out along the beach, sitting in his chair beside his fishing pole, squinting at the horizon.

He always knew when she was coming, although he pretended to be surprised each and every time.

"How's the fishing today?" Lena asked as she always did.

"Terrible. Just terrible. It's been awful today."

That was his standard answer. But she'd be willing to bet he had some fish on the string that he had staked in the shallow part of the lake.

"I brought you a casserole."

"I'm not interested in no charity," Joe said, sounding gruff and irritable, but Lena knew that was just a front. He was actually a rather nice fellow.

Maybe nice was a bit of an exaggeration, but Joe was softer than he looked. Softer than he sounded. Although she wouldn't consider him easy or even friendly. In fact, he was decidedly unfriendly.

But that didn't deter her.

"This is the one that you like so much that I made two weeks ago."

"Eat too much of something and you get sick of it," Joe said, and Lena figured he was just making conversation, because his eyes lit up at the casserole in her hands.

"I'm gonna take it in, and I'm gonna put it on your counter." She knew when she took it in, she would find the casserole dish she'd taken him last week, and it would be filled with the espresso beans.

It was a good thing she liked them.

She probably liked them a little bit too much. She had mentioned to Joe that they were addicting, and the very next time she came, Joe had more. Ever since, anytime she had taken a container, Joe had washed it and filled it with espresso beans.

He claimed they came from his son in Chicago.

The son Lena had never met. She had thought he was never around, but apparently he visited weekly.

She set the casserole down, glancing around the house and seeing that nothing much had changed. It was still sparsely furnished, and clean, but dingy inside. There weren't many windows. Grateful that her house at least allowed the sunlight in, because she didn't think she could live without it, she grabbed the container with the espresso beans in it and walked back out.

"See you found the beans," Joe said as he saw her carrying her dish back down.

"You know, I love these. But it's like you feed my addiction. I should probably stop."

Joe nodded. "Addictions are bad. You probably should."

"But thank you. I love them."

Under Joe's bushy eyebrows, his eyes glowed, and she knew that he loved hearing that he was doing something that made her happy.

It was a human characteristic almost to a person. People liked to make other people happy.

Of course, there were exceptions, but those were few and far between, and Joe wasn't one of them.

"Someday, I'm going to meet your son," she said conversationally.

"He doesn't visit nearly enough."

"He must come weekly."

"He should be here every day."

"But he works in Chicago."

"He can quit his job. He's made enough money to support a hundred people. He should move back out here where he belongs. The city ruins people. When you get out here, you can think for yourself, you don't have to follow the crowd. He gets brainwashed by idiots, and he loses his common sense."

On one of her visits, after she'd been visiting him for almost a year, Joe had told her that his two younger children had died in a car accident together. His wife had been driving, and she held herself responsible, even though another car ran a red light and T-boned the passenger side of her car, killing both of her children.

She had never recovered.

Now, it was just Joe and the mysterious son who lived in Chicago.

"I guess maybe we just need to be where we're supposed to be. That's the best place to find joy." She was not necessarily disagreeing with Joe. After all, she couldn't imagine being happy in the city, but some people were. Just as people who lived in the city might find it difficult to believe that someone could be happy in a town as small as Strawberry Sands.

"That's a bunch of blather. Kids should be home where they belong. Shouldn't run off to the big city getting sucked into the lies they tell," Joe mumbled, like he was annoyed because he thought she was defending his son.

"I guess I'm not a very good one to talk. All of my kids live pretty close to me. And that's a blessing, but it does make for more work too." She thought about the pancakes that she made this morning. It was after she'd made breakfast for all the guests at her bed-and-breakfast.

She didn't mind at all, and especially in the winter when guests were few and far between, she really appreciated having the visits.

The relationships with people were more important than complaining about the work involved.

Not to mention, God had given her so much, it was only right that she gave back. Even if it was to her family.

Or to a neighbor up the beach living in a lighthouse.

Of course, it wasn't like she served him and he didn't give her anything in return. Although, even if he didn't give her espresso beans, she would still bring him food.

"You call me if you need anything, okay?" she said, like she always did.

"Not gonna need nothing," the man said, looking out into the lake like he didn't care whether she left or not.

In the winter, she'd stay longer. Sometimes he'd be in the lighthouse, and she'd sit down and visit.

He didn't do much fishing when it was cold out. But she suspected that the fish were all he had to eat.

In the winter, she made sure that she brought him enough food to last a week.

Sometimes she walked up the beach twice.

It got pretty cold, but it wasn't like it was a dangerous walk or even that the terrain was very difficult. She just dressed warmly and set out.

"I'll see you next Tuesday," she said cheerfully as she waved at his scowling face.

He put a hand up, almost as though he could barely be bothered to say goodbye to her. But she knew that he appreciated her visits. She was sure of it.

She walked back down the beach, praying that God would watch over him, because the man was so alone.

Chapter 13

Kristin walked into the smell of yeasty bread. She smiled. She loved being home. What a stressful morning.

"Hey there, Gram," Luke said as he came out of the kitchen and saw them standing in the entryway taking their shoes off.

He glanced in the kitchen, as though making sure he knew where the girls were, and then he walked out down the hall to where they were.

Kristin had to admit her heart warmed at the idea that he wanted to be with them. There was concern in his eyes.

"Was everything okay?" he asked, looking grim and then raising his brows at her.

She thought he was truly worried. Or at least concerned. He didn't look like he was biting his nails or anything. It's just that he... He cared. That's what it was, and that made her smile.

Before she could answer, Gram said, "They just wanted to stick me again. They didn't take enough blood the first time, so they got their leeches out and stuck them on again. I'll tell you what, they killed George Washington that way, and it will kill me too." Gram stood slowly, and then as much as she could, she stomped down the hall muttering, "And it smells like I missed bread-baking day. Which is really sad because I love making bread. I hope that they save some jobs for me. I just might have to make my own." And she disappeared inside the kitchen.

"Wow. She's in rare form."

"Actually, that's probably common form," Kristin said with a small laugh. "Her white blood count was high. Exceptionally so. They took some more blood and then scheduled her for some tests. I am sorry that this was unexpected. And the rest of my week is probably up in the air since I'm not sure exactly how long these things are going to take. I already have the app downloaded, and once they have everything scheduled, I should be able to go in there and see what's going on."

"That's fine. Don't worry about it. We'll take care of Gram. And whatever time is left, we'll squeeze in what we need to do. I... I wanted to talk to you about what I saw in Rita's house." He lowered his voice, and she strained to hear.

"That bad?"

He nodded. "I wouldn't say it's an emergency to get her out, but... I would say it's pretty close."

"All right. I guess it never rains but it pours."

"I'm sorry you're feeling overwhelmed," he said, and she loved that he cared and the idea that he would do something if he could. "Why don't you go relax somewhere, and we'll finish baking bread?"

"Well, that's just it, while I was on my way home, Chi called me and said that someone was in the diner asking if she knew anyone who might want two twin beds."

"That's awesome. Because we do."

"That's exactly what I said. So she gave me the number of the person, and I called. They're not far outside of town, and I told him that maybe we could go to look at them and possibly pick them up this afternoon?" She grimaced, in an apologetic way, so that he knew that she wasn't trying to make his life more difficult but wanted to jump on the cheap beds while she could.

"That's perfect. I don't know how long the bread needs to rise, but I heard the ladies saying that it was almost time to let it sit for a while. Maybe we can go get the beds, come back to the bread, and then... Is there something we need to do to get rooms ready?"

She realized that with a mom who owned a bed-and-breakfast, he'd probably done his share of getting rooms ready.

"I think we'll be fine. If we have much time, I'd love to go through and clean them from top to bottom. But sweeping them, scrubbing floors, and getting the worst of the dust is probably the best we can do. I can throw the curtains in the washer and then meet you in the kitchen."

"That sounds great. I'll figure out how much longer we have, and maybe you can let the folks know what our ETA would be."

It turned out that they were able to get the beds and come back and do the bread just like they thought. The beds weren't the best thing that Kristin had ever seen, but she'd slept on worse, and they came with box springs and mattresses which looked to be in fairly good condition. The folks that were selling them said they were brand-new, but Kristin had doubts about that.

Regardless, the house was clean, and the mattresses would work for the girls. She was dying of curiosity to know what had gone on with Luke, what had made him think that it was such an emergency to get Rita and Becky under their roof.

When they pulled back in with the beds, the ladies had the bread in the oven, and the house smelled divine.

"Are we going to get to eat it?" Rita asked, holding tight to Becky's hand.

Becky was an adorable big sister, protecting her little sister, bossing her around, and half the time fighting with her, half the time acting like she was a china doll that would break if anyone even looked at her the wrong way.

"We sure are," Luke said as his stomach growled.

The girls giggled, Luke made a face, and Kristin's heart flipped just watching them.

It almost felt like they really could be a family.

Luke's phone went off, and he checked it.

His face registered shock, and then he looked abashed.

"There's something I forgot to tell you." He looked at Kristin.

"Okay?" Kristin said.

Luke looked back at the girls. "Why don't you guys run to the kitchen and see if the bread's out of the oven?"

He didn't have to tell them twice, and they ran off, holding hands and bumping each other down the hall.

Kristin smiled as they left, but she had a nagging concern about whatever it was that had made Luke make those faces.

"I forgot to tell you that...I bought a dog."

"You *bought* a dog?" Kristin said, emphasizing the word "bought."

"Well, such as it was." He cleared his throat, clearly uncomfortable, as he shifted from one foot to the other.

"So... Why did you do that?" Kristin asked, and then she looked around. "And where is it?" Had he put it in the house and not told her about it? Not that she had something against animals in the house. Not really. At least she didn't think she did. She supposed she preferred that they be clean. And free of whatever kind of critters animals carried around with them at times.

"Um. Well, anyway. Rita wasn't living in the best of conditions, and there was a dog on the premises. It... He was in pretty sad shape too. I was going to offer to just take him for the day, and then somehow, I ended up offering to buy him from the dude for a hundred bucks. He took me up on it."

"He sold his family pet?" Kristin asked, disbelief lacing every word. How did someone sell their dog?

"Seems like he'd prefer the hundred bucks, although he was pretty concerned about whether it was counterfeit or not."

"Did you tell him you had a printing press in your basement?"

"That'd be pretty tough, considering I don't have a basement. But no. I told him that I got it that morning from someone who bought hay off me. Which was the truth."

"I see. So... Where is the dog?" she asked, confused. If he bought the dog, did he leave without it?

"Well, it had fleas. I saw them." He bit his lip. "I actually looked Rita over pretty good while she was in my truck, because I didn't really figure that you wanted fleas in your house, and she said the dog was her best friend. Although, I'm pretty sure they kept it outside."

"I see. So you don't think Rita had fleas?" Kristin tried not to be too horrified. Fleas were not the worst thing that could happen to a person. Probably anyway. She couldn't think of too many other things she'd rather not have in her house. A rhinoceros maybe.

But it did give her a glimmer of the reason that Luke had said that it was an emergency to get Rita out of that house.

"No. I don't think she did. And I dropped the dog off at my sister's who is a dog groomer. You know Elinor."

"Oh. I forgot. So that was her texting you that he's ready?" she guessed. They'd gone a very circuitous route in order to figure out what in the world was going on.

"Yeah. Exactly. She said the dog was done, and she offered to drop him off, since her next client doesn't come in for another thirty minutes or so."

"Okay. We have some bread to offer her."

"She'll probably take us up on it," he said. "Thanks for not making a big deal about it. I really am sorry for not saying anything to you. I… First of all, I'm not really used to not just making decisions on my own, but I really didn't mean to offer to buy him. I guess I was thinking about taking him for the day, and I offered a hundred dollars, then when the dude seemed to think that I was offering him a hundred dollars to take him forever, I… I really wanted to."

"And that makes perfect sense to me," Kristin said, meaning it. She actually really loved the fact that Luke had had a heart for the dog and had wanted to save it. Along with Rita.

"I have another small problem."

"And that is?"

"You saw what Rita is wearing, it's just a thin little nighty. That's all she has. She didn't bring a package of clothes, or change, or anything. And… My mom said she probably needed everything. She emphasized the 'everything,' and I think that might mean that she needs undergarments."

Kristin tried not to laugh. Luke looked adorable with his cheeks heating and his one hand shoved behind his head scratching his neck.

"All right. She's staying tonight?"

"No. She's supposed to go home by the time they go to bed, but he didn't mention when that was. I'm guessing it's pretty late. They didn't seem like the early to bed, early to rise kind of people."

"I'm sure they're probably not," Kristin said, not judging, just agreeing. He wasn't really making a statement about what time the family went to bed. He was making more of a statement about how industrious the family seemed. People could work at night just as well as they could work during the day. But some people didn't work at all. And she caught that from what he was saying.

"Do you think their job is fostering children?" she asked, hoping that she was so far out in left field that she wasn't even close to the truth.

"It wouldn't shock me if that's their only source of income. So, getting Rita out of there probably is only going to lead to a bad situation for someone else."

"How do they pass the caseworker's inspection?" Kristin asked, more to herself than expecting Luke to answer for her.

"I think they are so desperate for foster parents that they will approve almost anyone. Anyone who seems like they care. I don't know. I really don't know much about the system, but I think we're going to learn more."

"Unless the person who's pulling strings for us keeps us away from that. Which I can only hope they do. I've never met a state system that I was happy to be acquainted with."

He laughed a little. "I could agree fervently with that."

"Do you think we could keep her longer?" Kristin asked, already trying to think of how they could keep from sending Rita back to such a place. She didn't need to see it to see the horror on Luke's face which said that anyone who would send their child somewhere with just a nighty on and nothing else wasn't the kind of person that he would want raising his daughter.

"I can text them and ask. We can see how long we can keep her. I can talk to my mom, and she can see if she can facilitate things with Becky and ask about Rita. But..."

"We need to be married," Kristin said, knowing immediately what he was going to say. He nodded.

"All right. And the sooner we can, the better. This week if possible."

"Maybe we should look it up. I don't even know if there's a waiting period in Michigan. It's not like I've ever gotten married before." He pulled his phone out as he spoke with his fingers flying over the screen.

In her head, Kristin was trying to figure out how this might fit into the plans that they had and the things that were going on with her grandma. She said a quick prayer that things with her grandma were not serious.

"A three-day waiting period," Luke said.

"Then we should probably go apply today, and then we can get it by Friday."

"Sounds good." He clicked his phone off and shoved it into his back pocket. "I texted my sister and told her to bring the dog here. We can eat bread, get the dog, go get the marriage license, then come back and put the beds together. This is turning out to be a pretty busy day."

She laughed. "I have a feeling that life is about to get a lot crazier for us. You already know that I have my gram to take care of, and of course I have to look after Miss Alma and Miss Joyce and Miss Daisy. What about you? Do you have things that you need to do?" She had no idea what was going on with the farm or anything. They hadn't really talked about that at all.

"Other than taking the girls for a horse ride today, I had the day off."

"I totally forgot about that. Do you think we'll be able to squeeze that in?"

"I don't know. Maybe. I think we should try. Even if we don't get the beds together. We can put a tent up in the yard or something. I think I have one at my mom's house somewhere in the garage."

"That would be fun for them, I think. And it would be safe in the backyard. It's fenced."

"And Bruno... Maybe we can change his name."

"That's his name?" She couldn't remember whether he had used it before or not. If he had, she totally missed it.

"Yep. Bruno. Very clichéd, and very apropos."

She laughed, although she supposed if she could see where Bruno had come from, she probably wouldn't be laughing.

"Maybe we should check with Rita and see what she says. She might be attached to the name."

"She's definitely attached to the dog."

"If he's her best friend, I would say she probably is."

She realized that in the last week or so, she and Luke had gone from antagonistic toward each other to having an entire conversation where they didn't fight once. In fact, they were laughing together and trying to help each other out.

"You never said if you had more to do on the farm?"

"I just got the second cutting of hay in. I'll have to do the third cutting soon, but not for a week or so. In that amount of time, I should be able to get everything done that we need to get done here. And if we don't put the beds together and instead put up a tent for the girls to sleep in tonight, or we could take them to my mom's house?"

"Whichever works for me. I think I prefer the tent idea, but I know your mom loves having them too."

"She has her own day. And this one is mine. I'm not sure who Becky goes to tomorrow, but we might be able to keep her. Especially since the town knows that we're..."

"Getting married in order to adopt her?" Kristin said, when he didn't seem to be able to find the words.

"Yeah. It is...getting a little bit real. We're talking about getting licenses and going this afternoon and... I guess I ought to think about moving my things here. There's a lot."

"Yes. After we eat our bread, I can walk up and show you the rooms."

"All right. You know what, let's not get stressed about this. We'll just take it as it comes."

"I like that," she said, smiling at him.

"In the meantime, that bread smells really good."

She could tell from the sounds in the kitchen that the oven had been opened and closed several times, and it sounded like they'd set the pans down on the stovetop.

"Shall we go see if we can get a few bites before it's gone?" she asked, smiling.

"Let's do that." He held his hand up, and she wasn't exactly sure what he meant, but she slipped hers into it, and that's how they walked down the hall, side by side, with their hands clasped together. It made her feel like they were facing life together, and that felt good.

Chapter 14

"Does Bruno get to ride a horse too?"

"Don't be silly. How is he going to hold the reins?"

Rita scrunched her nose like she hadn't thought about that, and Luke exchanged a glance with Kristin over their heads. They smiled at each other as the girls continued to discuss it, with Becky taking turns being a normal big sister, irritated with her little sister, and then suddenly shifting into overprotective mode.

It was like she couldn't decide whether she wanted to be irritated, or whether she just wanted to enjoy the time with her sister.

In a way that made Luke sad, but in another way he figured that if nothing else, the time apart from her sister taught Becky to appreciate the time they had together. He could see her struggling with pushing aside her selfishness to give Rita whatever she wanted.

As he looked back in front of them toward the beach, he saw the Great Pyrenees standing off to the side as though watching them. It had seemed to be making appearances more and more often in his life.

It seemed a little bit odd that as he and Kristin got together, he saw the dog more and more.

It stood back, almost as though it knew that Bruno might not appreciate his company.

At some point Luke wanted to ask someone around town about it, whose it was and whether it was being taken care of, but he kept forgetting. At the very least he wanted to talk to Kristin. Although, if they were going to get married, adopt two girls, and a dog, they probably weren't going to have room for yet another dog.

He needed to be reasonable.

The girls were still chatting as they reached the stable and he went out to the pasture with Becky to catch the horses.

Becky had learned a lot from working at Davis's stable, and she was able to lead the first horse in and tie it up. As he brought the second horse in, he noticed that Becky was showing both Rita and Kristin how to groom the first horse before they checked it out.

He gave her some words of praise, shared another look with Kristen, and went back out to catch the last two horses.

By the time they had everyone saddled up, and the girls mounted, they were just in time to make it for the sunset.

They had gotten a couple of bombproof horses that he put the girls on, so he was comfortable with them riding ahead, even though Becky, who had been working at Matt's stable for a good while, was almost what he would consider an accomplished horsewoman.

"It was quite a day," he said as his horse settled into stride beside Kristin's.

"It was a good day," she said, her eyes had a happy glow, as a smile lingered around her lips.

His eyes got caught on those lips for just a minute, before he looked out over the lake, as the sun glowed orange on the water.

"I agree. It's kind of hard to believe that this is our life."

"On days like today, it's hard to believe that there's anything that could ever upset it. Like, arguments or disagreements, or red tape, or having the state tell us no."

"I don't want to borrow trouble. So far, whoever's been pulling the strings for us, has done a good job. And, Rita's foster parents are allowing her to stay for three nights, so I can't complain about that either."

"If they thought that we were thinking about adopting her, they might have changed their mind." Kristin looked at him with her brows lifted as though asking if he would agree with that statement.

He nodded. "I think they thought I was crazy for wanting her to begin with. But, I also think that sometimes kids wear you down, and you appreciate a break. I guess I wouldn't be too hard on them."

"I have to agree with that. I know it's the way the ladies are sometimes." Kristin looked away as she spoke, almost as though she were ashamed she was admitting it.

"It's okay to admit you get tired."

"I know. But, we're talking about my grandma. And, I don't want her to think that I don't want her with me. I would feel terrible if she decided that she would rather be in a nursing home, and only did that because she thought she was doing me a favor. Truly, most of the time I love it."

"I think everybody understands that." He felt like she needed to understand that people didn't judge her for needing a break. Everyone did at times. He figured there would be plenty of times where they would need a rest from the kids and from the ladies and from the things that wore them down.

"This is a good break," Kristin said, more cheerfulness in her voice and less worry.

"It sure is. There's just something rejuvenating about the lake, and even more so when it's the lake at sunset."

"Or sunrise." She smiled, and he returned it, thinking about their early morning meeting. It felt like so long ago.

They had applied for their marriage license, but it wouldn't be good for three days. That was the waiting period. But they'd already arranged for the preacher to marry them, and he'd already spoken with his mother. She was going to talk to her contact, and see what they could work out with the girls.

"We will probably have a visit from a caseworker in the near future."

"I know. And I think I'm comfortable with that. I mean, they don't expect the house to be spotlessly clean, do they? Is controlled chaos okay? Maybe laughter and the smell of food in the kitchen would go further than it being spotlessly clean, right?"

"I think so. Maybe the idea that we know what's going on with the school. I texted Fred Belzer, who was the superintendent at Blueberry Beach. He is going to email me the schedule. I'm guessing that the first day of school isn't too far away."

August was drawing to a close, and already the breeze felt cooler than it had all summer.

"I hadn't even thought about school."

"That's why there's two of us. So hopefully between us, we can think of everything. After all, I didn't really think too much about food, but I know you've got something waiting for us when we get home."

"Well that's an area where the ladies can help. They all like to cook to varying degrees. So as long as we can keep up with the groceries, we should at least keep the girls fed."

"Fed, a roof over their heads, and make sure they go to school." He lifted his shoulder. "I feel like we have most things in hand."

"Close. We grabbed a few things today when we picked up the marriage license, but we're going to need to do something about Rita's wardrobe."

"Maybe we can figure out how to ask her if she has more clothes at her foster parent's house."

"If they fit her like that nighty, I would say that we can just forget about them. It seems like she might've had a growth spurt over the summer."

The girls were squabbling, with Becky telling Rita that she was just a little baby, and she didn't know anything, and she needed to be quiet and listen.

"I guess we're going to be hearing a lot of that." Kristin sounded sad, like she hated to hear people argue.

"If things work out the way we hope they do, right?" he asked, and then he thought maybe he'd better clarify. "You know, we can just do one girl. We don't have to try to adopt Rita. If you think it's going to be too much."

"No. I don't think it's going to be too much. And, I'm sorry I sounded a little bit... I don't know..."

"Sad?"

"Maybe. But it wasn't because I didn't want to have the girls fighting. I guess it was more because I didn't have siblings to fight with. If I had had time with siblings, I like to think that with the wisdom that I have now, I would have enjoyed every second. And I wouldn't have wasted any of it arguing."

He shifted in the saddle, and then finally decided that he was going to say what her words brought to his mind.

"All right. Let's do this," he started. That made her head turn over toward him, but her eyes lit up with interest.

"Yeah?" she said.

"Let's pretend that you've gotten to the end of your life, and you never got married."

She tilted her head a little, thinking about where he was going, and trying to figure it out.

"Okay?"

"All right, now let's say that you see a married couple fighting, and you think to yourself, that's sad, because I spent my whole life unmarried. If I had the opportunity to have a husband, I certainly wouldn't waste any time arguing with him."

"Oh my goodness. I see where you're going with this. That is sneaky." She laughed, and patted her horse's neck, as the sky exploded over their heads in orange and pink and blues and even some shades of green.

She shook her head, but she said, "You know what. You're so right. I was just sitting there thinking how I wanted to correct them, and I never even thought about how I could apply it to myself. But you're spot on. I will try, as hard as I can, to not waste any of our married life fighting with you. As long as you agree with everything I say."

He laughed, then shook his head. "I don't think that's how this is supposed to work."

"I know."

"But I do think that most disagreements are because of selfishness. We want our way, we want other people to do what we think they should do. Instead of just being content with what we have and working on improving ourselves. We're always working on improving other people and fighting for what we want."

"Like I was just doing," she said, looking a little abashed.

"We all do it. I do too. I think about how everyone else can improve, and I neglect to look at myself and realize that improvement needs to start with me."

"Maybe we ought not to be too hard on ourselves though, because things are going to be a lot different in both of our lives."

"Yeah," he drew the word out a little bit, because he actually wanted to talk to her about exactly how different things were going to be. As in, what exactly were they expecting out of their marriage?

Maybe that was something they could talk about later.

It turned out that it was full dark by the time they got the horses back to the stable, unsaddled and rubbed down.

Luke had considered going to the diner for some dessert, or at least some ice cream, but it seemed like it was bedtime.

Kristin agreed, and they reluctantly walked home. The evening had been so nice and relaxing after their full and eventful day, that he hated to see it end.

"Can I have Bruno in the tent with me?" Rita asked eagerly.

"No! We don't let dogs sleep with us," Becky said, sounding very bossy.

"Well, Becky. I know that you're used to making all the decisions yourself, but I think whether or not the dog can sleep with you will be Kristin and my decision." Luke tried not to be too forceful. He didn't want to have a head-on confrontation with Becky, but she needed to understand that she wasn't the boss of the family. Of course, she was used to being her own boss, and he figured that it was going to be a little touchy to get her to submit to parental authority. Maybe she never really would. And he might have to accept that.

That was something else he probably should talk to Kristin about. How they were going to parent a child who was used to making her own decisions, living by herself, and keeping herself alive. It might be impossible to get her to go back to being a child. And, it might be counterproductive to do it as well. After all, they didn't want her to regress. But, she acted too old for her age.

He sighed, not sure where to draw the line with that. He figured it probably wasn't going to be the last thing that gave him fits.

Lord? Are you sure I'm up for this?

Then he remembered that he had Kristin beside him. It wasn't just him.

"I don't want a dog in the tent," Becky said, sounding belligerent.

"I think it'll make Rita feel safer to have Bruno in the tent with her. And I sent him to my sister who cleaned him up and made sure that he's not going to give you any kind of critters."

"I don't care. Dogs are dirty."

"I want him!"

"We can make sure that Bruno just sleeps on Rita's side. Will that work for you Becky?" Kristin asked, and her tone didn't sound overly commanding either. Maybe she figured out what he already had, and that was that Becky was going to take a little bit of careful handling if they didn't want her to run away from their home as well.

He wasn't sure that there was any kind of roadmap for the situation that they were dealing with.

"But I don't want him on my side." Becky's words were firm, but at least Kristin was able to get her to allow the dog in the tent.

"That's fine. Although, if Becky doesn't want to sleep with the dog, maybe you two aren't going to be able to share a room like you wanted to." He figured he'd just throw that out there. Because the girls had insisted that they wanted to have the same bedroom.

He thought that maybe the caseworker would want to see that they were separated, but maybe they just wanted to know there were enough bedrooms in case the girls wanted to be in separate rooms, they could accommodate that.

There were so many unknowns. So many things he wasn't sure about. He felt like he was walking a narrow path, one he couldn't see.

"The dog stays outside. No dogs in the house," Becky said.

"But I want Bruno to stay with me. He's never been allowed inside the house before, but he's a good house dog. I know he is," Rita said, and in the light of Luke's phone, she buried her head in Bruno's fur as he lay down beside her.

She snuggled her body against his, and Luke's heart twisted. The poor girl, the thing she loved most in the entire world was a mangy old dog.

At least the dog seemed to love her as well, since he hadn't left her side since his sister had brought it back.

"If you girls need anything, I'll be right inside the house, okay?"

"I'm going to go home, but Kristin can call me if anything goes wrong."

"What's going to go wrong?" Becky asked, hiding a yawn. "Strawberry Sands is as safe as a town can be." She said that like she knew it. And Luke figured she probably did.

They said their prayers, and then Luke and Kristin backed out from the opening of the tent, allowing the flap to fall down.

"When I picked up the tent and told mom that I wanted to see if we would be able to try to adopt the kids, and have it be expedited if we could, she didn't give me too much hassle, because she knew I was in a hurry. But I'm pretty sure the next time I see her, she's going to want the answers to a lot of questions."

Kristin laughed, almost as though she were enjoying his discomfort. Or maybe commiserating with him. "I don't have a mom, so I really don't have to worry about that."

They walked up the porch steps, and he opened the door for her. Thinking that maybe they'd go in and sit down at the table for a little bit and he'd be able to talk to her.

But Kristin had barely stepped in the house before her gram stepped in front of her, with her gram's three friends flanking her in the hall.

"We need to talk to you two," her gram said, her hands on her hips.

"You don't have a mom," he murmured. And, like he figured, Kristin chuckled.

But, he thought maybe the next few minutes, or possibly longer, were going to be uncomfortable.

"You two can just march yourselves right into the kitchen. We've got a few questions we need to ask you," Miss Daisy said, looking for all the world like Kristin was her daughter, instead of a woman she just started living with.

"We'll answer any questions you want us to," Luke said, sounding casual. He wasn't really concerned. He didn't want the ladies to be angry with him, but he hadn't done anything wrong.

He'd barely even held her hand. He hadn't kissed her. He certainly wasn't worried that they were going to ask them any questions that he was afraid - or ashamed - to answer.

"You sure will, sonny," Miss Alma said, waiting until they walked by her, before clomping behind them with her walker. Miss Joyce followed along, and there was a lot of clomping in the hall before they reached the kitchen.

Somehow that sounded more ominous to Luke than the threat of having them talk to him. But, maybe he was underestimating the situation. He hoped not.

Chapter 15

Kristin tried to keep from smiling. Luke sat down at the table next to her. She had deliberately taken a chair at the side of the table, so that he could either sit at the head, which might give him more of an illusion of control, or, he could sit beside her.

She loved that he had chosen the seat beside her, and, when he sat down, he put his arm behind her chair, giving even more of a picture of them as a team.

She liked that. Liked that she wasn't facing the ladies alone. They could be intimidating at times. Especially when they all ganged up together, as it appeared that they were doing now.

"How long have you known Kristin?" Miss Joyce began the interrogation.

"All my life, pretty much," Luke answered easily. He looked at her, and she met his gaze. "Is that right?"

"I'm pretty sure we were in the church nursery together." That was when her mom had been visiting her aunt, the one that eventually raised her after her mom died, but the ladies didn't need to know that it wasn't a full-time thing.

And sure enough, that comment took the wind out of Miss Joyce's sails.

"Okay, so I understand that you guys know each other, but it's my understanding that you haven't been friends for very long." Daisy crossed her arms over her chest and looked over the top of her glasses at both of them.

Kristin managed to keep from squirming. It helped that Luke's hand lifted from the back of her chair and came down lightly on her shoulder. Warm and reassuring.

"I think sometimes when people are attracted to each other, and they're fighting that attraction, it looks like they don't get along at all. But in reality, they're just trying to run away from the inevitable."

That was a good answer. Kristin wanted to turn to Luke and congratulate him on coming up with a great response, but she figured that might ruin the picture he was trying to present.

So she didn't say anything.

She did, however, lift her hand up, and touched his fingers where they lay on her shoulder. He moved them just slightly, and their fingers threaded, clasping and giving them a link that bound them together.

She liked the way that felt.

"Luke is right. We had a near-death experience together, and both of us had a tendency to blame the other person. We talked that out, and realized that both of us needed to take responsibility for our actions, and that removed the issues that lay between us. I... I think Luke is pretty awesome, and I always have."

There, she hopefully bolstered his case.

Miss Alma's brows went up, then she nodded begrudgingly. "I've heard of that type of thing. Once people get over their animosity toward each other, they find out they really like each other. But do you two have anything in common?"

"We both love the girls," Kristin said immediately.

Luke nodded in agreement. "We definitely have the girls bringing us together. But we both love Strawberry Sands, we both love horseback rides on the beach, and we're both committed to making our marriage work."

"We both like to eat. There's that."

She and Luke laughed together, because although they never discussed it, that was one thing they had in common.

"We both like strawberries," Luke added and they shared another smile.

"I think you two have an answer to everything," her grandma said, looking thoughtfully at her. Then, to Kristin's surprise, her grandma looked at her friends.

"When I was looking around Strawberry Sands trying to find someone who was perfect for my granddaughter, Luke was the man I kept landing on. Part of it was because I could tell that my granddaughter was more interested in him than she was in the other men in Strawberry Sands, but part of it was because I just had a feeling he was right for her. I can't even put my finger on why. But, as much time as I've spent trying to get the two of them together, I didn't expect it to happen quite like this." She looked back at Luke and Kristin. "But I can't say that I'm disappointed, or that I think that you two should wait. You've obviously talked about this, and you're both adults. I think we should allow you to do exactly what you plan." She looked at her friends. "I'm going to bed."

And with that, she turned and walked out of the kitchen, effectively ending what Kristin had feared was going to be a very long night.

After a few moments of stunned silence, Alma, Joyce and Daisy looked at each other, murmured their agreement, bid them good night, and filed out of the kitchen as well.

Sooner than she anticipated, Kristin found herself sitting in the kitchen alone with Luke. Their hands were still joined, and he still had his arm around the back of her chair, as they sat side-by-side.

"Well, that didn't quite go the way I had anticipated," Luke said, breaking the silence that settled in the kitchen after the ladies had left.

"I was afraid you were going to be upset about that." She appreciated that not only was he not upset, but he seemed like the whole thing had amused him.

"I guess I don't see any reason to get upset," he said, sounding a little confused as to why she would think he would be.

"I guess a lot of times people don't like other people questioning their motives."

"I suppose that's true. And I guess I don't like it anymore than anyone else, but it just doesn't seem like something to get upset about.. Those ladies were only questioning us because they care about you. Shouldn't that make me happy? Especially since... I care about you too."

She wasn't sure why that surprised her, but it did. She couldn't stop her eyes from widening.

"I don't think it should surprise you that I care about you. That's okay, isn't it?" He leaned a little closer to her, and it almost felt like he was pulling her toward him, and she found herself leaning in his direction. Not much, just tilting toward him.

"Of course," she murmured and then, she took a breath. "I care about you too." When had that happened? Of course she'd always been... Interested in him. Attracted maybe. But, she found herself caring whether he was upset. Whether he was happy. Concerned about where he was and what he was doing. If he was hungry, or needed something. She found herself wanting to take care of him.

That probably wasn't something she could admit to just anyone. After all, that wasn't something a woman was supposed to want to do anymore. But, she definitely wanted that.

"I find myself thinking about you at the oddest times," he murmured, and his words sent a shiver down her spine. "Isn't that strange?" He seemed to be asking himself that just as much as he was asking her.

"You're doing better than me. I have a hard time not thinking about you." She tried to infuse a little bit of lightness into her words. The tension between them seemed heavy and thick and she wanted to ease it somehow. With a laugh, with a joke, or something, except... She wanted to know what else he was going to say.

"That makes me happy," he said, then his lips turned up. "It's good to know that you're struggling like I am."

His thumb brushed over her shoulder, and he squeezed her hand.

"I guess if we're getting married, it shouldn't be a struggle, should it?"

"I believe you're right."

Maybe it shouldn't matter, but it made her happy that he was able to admit that she might be right about something. She knew there were men who couldn't. Knew there were people who couldn't seem to make themselves admit that they might be wrong and someone else might be right.

"You know how we talked about giving up? Sacrificing? I'm wondering now if maybe what seemed like a sacrifice, was actually just God getting rid of things in my life so he could give me something even better." That thought was just forming in her head. Was it possible that she was going to marry someone she loved? Could she make the choice to love someone, but also have those tingly feelings that the world seemed to think a person needed in order to fall in love?

"I have to agree. It's looking less and less like a sacrifice, and more and more like a gift from God." He looked thoughtful. "I think that's the way the Lord often works. He just wants to see if we're willing to give up some things we think we need in order for him to bless us with something we never thought we'd want, but find ourselves craving once He offers it to us."

Was that true? Was her willingness to give up her nicely organized life in order to try to take in two girls and give them a home, going to end up being the thing that blessed her the most? That was so like God.

"I know that shouldn't surprise me, God is good like that all the time, but it really does. I... I wasn't expecting this."

"This?"

"To feel... Like you might be the very person that I always wanted to marry. I know it's a little soon to say for sure, but I love that you have integrity and character and that you're honest. That you're willing to step up and sacrifice."

"I think we just agreed that it's not really a sacrifice. It's more like I'm getting more than I ever thought I would. And, the more time I spend around those little girls, the more I want to get this moving so that they're ours for good. They... They grow on a person."

"It's okay. You can say you love them."

"I think I'm going to love my entire new family."

"Even the old ladies?"

His lips curved up. "Maybe especially the old ladies. Because they love you."

His words made her feel warm and happy all over, and she just wanted to sit and enjoy the feeling, but she remembered that perhaps Miss Heather could have something seriously wrong with her.

Maybe that showed on her face, because Luke's look of affection drew into concern.

"Your gram?"

She nodded.

"We'll just have to take what comes. We can pray, we can work, and then we trust God to do what's best for us."

"I know."

They sat there quietly for a moment and then she said, "Changing the subject, I feel like I should be with you whenever you talk to your mom. She might have the same kind of reaction that my gram and the other ladies had. It's not really fair that you have to face her alone, since I didn't."

"I hope we're not going to do tit for tat and everything has to be fair. That's not really life, is it?"

"No. It's not." And she appreciated that he understood that and wasn't looking for everything to be exactly right. That he might be willing to give a little more, and at times she had to be willing to do the same. "Still, I'm willing if you want me to." She paused. "Just to be with you."

That made his lips curve up again. "Wow. You'd face down my mother, who can be a very formidable woman, just to spend time with me? I feel like maybe this is getting a little more serious than what I suspected."

"You faced the ladies with me." She lifted her chin, liking how they were kind of skirting around the idea that maybe they were both starting to like each other more than just a little. They were getting married either way, but it was exciting to think that maybe there would be more between them than just a desire to help two little girls who needed them.

"It was fun. I... I found that it doesn't really matter what I'm doing, if I'm doing it with you, I enjoy it. Is that terrible?"

"That's a huge compliment, and I feel like I don't deserve it, because I can't imagine what there is about me that makes things more fun, but that definitely makes me happy. And, I could say the exact same thing about you. I look forward to being with you, no matter what we're doing. Even if it's just putting the girls to bed in the tent."

"Speaking of going to bed. It's probably time for me to leave. I'll go straight home, but I'll probably talk to my mom in the morning. Would you like to come?"

"Sure. I'll check with my gram to make sure that she can watch the girls, and we can go early."

"We can watch the sunrise on the beach, you can help me pack some things in my house, and we'll stop at mom's on our way here to bring the stuff."

"That sounds like a plan."

They stared at each other for just a little bit, then he leaned forward. She held her breath, but he put his lips on her forehead, pressing for just a moment and then whispering, "Thanks for a great day."

She was a little disappointed, but she also loved that he wasn't pushing for a physical side to the relationship. Hopefully it wasn't because he didn't want one, but more because he wanted to lay the groundwork with an intellectual connection before they moved on to anything else. After all, she had some big revelations tonight. That he liked her. That he thought about her. That he wanted to spend time with her. That... That their marriage might not be as much of a marriage of convenience as what she was thinking it had been.

Of course, if they had a regular relationship, they wouldn't even be thinking about getting married already, so that was a little unusual, but beyond that, she enjoyed the thought that she wasn't the only one who might be falling in love.

<h1 style="text-align:center">Chapter 16</h1>

It was still dark when Luke got out of bed in the morning.

He didn't bother to light a lamp, but grabbed his phone and pulled his Bible app up as he walked outside and stood on the porch of his cottage.

He'd lived there since his early twenties. Almost ten years. He loved it. Loved watching the sunsets in the evening, loved seeing the changing water during the different seasons of the year. He'd spent a lot of time talking to God on his front porch, contemplating the lake and the water and the way nature moved.

It made him a little bit sad to think about leaving it. But, he wasn't as sad as he was excited.

Last night he felt like Kristin and he were an actual couple. A romantic, we really like each other, kind of couple.

It'd been hard to go to sleep last night. He'd wanted to do more than kiss her forehead.

He thought she possibly wanted more too, but he also didn't want to move too fast. It seemed like a good idea to lay a solid foundation. After all, their relationship wasn't based on the cushy feelings of falling in love. It was based on mutual decisions, doing something that was best for two little girls, and making a commitment that neither one of them planned to break.

If they fell in love with each other, that was just extra.

It made him smile to think that, because his God was a God of extra.

He thought about the verse that talked about giving. Where God commanded a man to give, then said if he obeyed, men would give back, pressed down, shaken together and running over.

He thought about how when he was a kid, collecting rocks or shells on the beach, and he'd try to fit as many as he could into his bucket, pressing it down, filling it up with more until it was overflowing and shells fell out as he ran to his mom to show her what he had.

It made him smile to think of God giving to him like that.

And all he had to do was obey the command and give to begin with.

He had a feeling that God giving him Kristin was that type of gift. One that was pressed down, shaken together and running over. Because it was becoming obvious to him that Kristin wasn't a normal kind of girl. She was the kind of woman he'd been looking for. Funny she'd been under his nose all the time.

She was the kind of girl who thought about other people, and put them first. She wasn't afraid to work, but she knew how to have fun as well. Who could laugh, even when things weren't going well.

She'd gotten some bad news about her Gram yesterday, but she didn't allow that to ruin their night, didn't allow it to ruin her mood. That was so unusual.

She didn't make it the center of attention, or put herself and her cares and worries ahead of everything.

She hadn't suggested that they move the wedding back, or that they just put everything on hold until she got things straightened out. She accepted the fact that whatever was happening was from the Lord.

He could have looked high and low and not found a woman like that, and here God dropped one in his lap.

There was no way he was going to let her go. He was going to hold on tight, as tight as he could. As tight as she would let him. And just pray that he could be the kind of man a woman like that deserved.

Headlights flashed, even as the sky seemed to lighten just a little, and he smiled, feeling the anticipation dip in his stomach, and forcing his feet to remain planted until her car came to a stop.

He allowed himself to take the front steps in one leap as he jogged to her car and opened the door for her.

"My goodness, such service so early in the morning."

"She wakes up happy. I like it." Another thing to be thankful for. Morning wasn't always people's best times. Sometimes he woke up and didn't want to talk to anyone for an hour or two, until he got his bearings. Even if you didn't want to talk, though, he could still be nice. He'd been around people who couldn't. It was good to know that Kristen wasn't one of those people.

"Maybe part of my happiness was because I was coming here. I was looking forward to seeing you. I... Missed you after you left last night."

His whole heart smiled at her admission. It was a little shyly spoken like she wasn't quite sure whether they could pick up from where they'd left off last night. He liked that she was brave enough to try.

"I didn't exactly regret not kissing you, but I did spend some time last night wishing I would have." He held his hand out, and she put her hand in it, and their fingers threaded together as they stood beside the car, neither one of them making a move to walk toward his cottage.

"I spent a little time doing the same thing," she admitted.

The dusky light of dawn didn't allow color, but he didn't really need it. A world of shades of gray was enough to see the glow in her eyes as she looked up at him.

"It's kind of tempting to kiss you now so I don't spend the day wondering whether I can or not and looking for a good opportunity to do so."

"Or, I could take it out of your hands and just kiss you. And then that would save us both a lot of wondering."

"Oh no. You're not going to end up telling our kids that our first kiss was because of your bravery. After all, I'm supposed to be the brave one."

"It takes bravery to kiss me?" she asked, adding a little tease to her voice which made him smile, despite the tingle in his fingertips and the thumping of his heart in his chest.

"It takes bravery, because I'm not sure if you want to kiss me quite as bad as I want to kiss you. It takes a little bit more self-control to tell myself that I won't regret waiting."

"How long are we waiting?" she asked, and he smiled at the disappointment in her tone.

"We waited all night. Do we need to keep waiting?"

"No?"

He tugged on her hand, and she closed the gap between them with one step. Putting his arms around her, he leaned his forehead on hers, and said, "I spent more time last night thanking God for giving me the most amazing woman I've ever met, and the more I get to know you, the more I can't help but think God must really love me. After all, I never thought I would find anyone half as wonderful. And yet here you are."

His words made her smile broaden and she tilted her head up. Her arms wrapped around his waist and tugged just a little. He didn't need any further urging, but lowered his head, and touched her lips with his.

He wasted his time dreaming the night before, because kissing Kristin was far better than anything he'd thought about, and he found himself not wanting to pull away.

The sun was glowing orange on the water when he finally lifted his head, pleased to see that she was just as breathless as he was.

"I thought we would watch the sunrise together, I...have to admit I missed most of it. Although, I think kissing you definitely beats watching the sunrise."

"I agree," she said simply. And she tightened her arms around him, laying her head on his shoulder, as they both looked out at the water. Behind them the sun's rays touched everything with color, and the glassy surface of Lake Michigan reflected every changing hue.

He wasn't sure he'd ever seen a more glorious sunrise, but most likely, it was the knowledge that God loved him, loved him so much that he gave him a gift like Kristin.

They didn't need words to keep watching, but every once in a while, he dropped his head and touched his lips to her temple or her forehead or hair.

Maybe it was just to make sure she was still there. Or maybe it was just that his feelings needed that outlet. He didn't typically have too much trouble containing himself, but he found he wanted to touch her constantly.

That was going to make packing up his things a little bit difficult.

"Coffee?" he finally asked once the sun was well and truly up, and he knew they needed to get moving, or they weren't going to get anything accomplished. And they had a lot to do.

"No thank you. I can drink it, but I don't usually."

"I typically drink it more in the winter. But if you want some, just say so."

"No. I think kissing is better than coffee. At least for me."

"I think that's a compliment. I'll take it."

"It was definitely a compliment."

This temptation to forget they had work to do was strong, but he remembered how he had been thinking that it was best to take things slow anyway.

Reluctantly he said, "I have some boxes on the back porch, and I've already put my clothes into the suitcase I have. Anything that you don't need at your house can stay here. I'm not sure what we'll use the cottage for, but it's not like I need to clean it out."

She nodded against his chest, and she seemed as reluctant as he to pull back and focus on the business at hand.

But, Kristin had already proven that she was not just kind and compassionate but also responsible.

And he found that he had never worked with anyone he enjoyed working with more. They laughed and talked together, and had everything they needed packed up in no time. They agreed that they'd use the cottage as a fun getaway, so they left the dishes and plates which Kristin didn't need at her house anyway. They even talked about using it as a rental.

They hadn't talked much about finances, and he was making enough so that they would be comfortable, if not rich. He supposed the same was true for her. If they combined their households, and added a rental, it would stand to reason that they would be in good shape.

There was a part of him that wished to provide more, but there was a bigger part that knew that Kristin wouldn't care. She wasn't looking at him to provide wealth.

She wanted a man with integrity and character. And she saw that when she looked at him. That meant more to him then he could say, and made him appreciate her just that much more.

Breakfast was over and most of his mom's bed-and-breakfast guests had checked out when they walked up the walk to her front door.

She was sitting on the front porch, resting. She often did after the guests were gone and she had breakfast cleaned up, took a break before it was time to clean the rooms and be ready for the afternoon's check ins.

Maybe it was just his imagination, but his mom seemed a little older and a little more tired.

Maybe there were cares and concerns that she had that she hadn't been sharing with him. He'd been a little wrapped up in his own affairs lately.

And this was going to be a shock to her.

Too late he thought that maybe he should have tried to find an easier way to tell her.

Chapter 17

Lena watched Luke come up the walk with Kristin beside him. She smiled to herself. She had known for a long time that Luke and Kristin were perfect for each other. They just needed to see that.

Heather had a tendency to push them apart, but maybe that was part of God's plan too. Maybe they just needed to stay apart until the time was right for them to come together.

She noted that Luke held Kristin's hand as they came up the walk. He said something low, and Kristin looked up, concern in her eyes.

Then she smiled reassuringly, and Lena could almost see the tension drain out of her son's shoulders. His face relaxed, and he smiled back at Kristin.

It warmed Lena's heart to see the exchange.

"Good morning. You two look rather happy this morning."

"It's been a good morning so far. Did you see the sunrise?" Luke asked, coming up and leaning down to kiss her cheek.

She put a hand on his shoulder, wrapped him in a short hug, and then gave a quick hug to Kristin who leaned down and bussed her cheek as well.

"I did. I actually took a walk on the beach before sunrise, and it was beautiful on the way back."

The days were getting shorter, the breeze chillier, and winter would be coming soon. She didn't really mind. She enjoyed days of snuggling beside the fire, warm blankets and flickering candles, the holidays and soups and all the things that came with winter.

At least now, the boys took care of the farm and she didn't have to worry about frozen water lines, animals that needed to be fed in the middle of snowstorms, and the house that constantly needed to be cleaned, especially if it was to be suitable for guests.

Her life was definitely easier than it used to be.

More lonely, as well.

For some reason Kristin's cheek seemed to heat at the mention of the sunrise. Which made Lena wonder what in the world could be causing embarrassment over a topic so innocent.

"You two aren't usually so happy together," she commented, when neither of them said anything.

"We decided to get married," Luke said.

He wasn't joking. She was sure of that. Luke was not her child that had a tendency to mess with her. That would be Ryan.

Ryan was a whole different ball game, and one she didn't want to think about right now. He wasn't happy with his life, and she wasn't sure what she as his mom could do to fix that. Because of course she wanted to. She wanted all of her children to be happy. But, that had to be something they came to on their own. It couldn't be something she did for them. Unfortunately, Ryan was taking a little longer than the others to figure out his place in life. It made her sad.

"I don't think you're kidding," she said, with a smile. "Congratulations. I always knew you two were meant for each other."

Luke stared at her like he had expected her to say something completely different.

"That's it?" he finally said.

Kristin laughed a little. "He was afraid he was going to shock you. I told him that mothers usually know."

"I think you're wise, Kristin. And I think you're getting an excellent man." She turned to her son. "And you are getting an amazing woman. I know you're going to take care of her. This match makes me very happy." She smiled, allowing them to see on her face that her words were true. She couldn't have put two better people together had she tried. As long as Luke could get along with Heather. But she felt that now that he was a little bit more mature than he used to be, he probably could.

"You don't even look surprised," Luke said, like he still hadn't quite gotten over the fact that he wasn't having to talk her into anything.

"Would it make you feel more comfortable if I acted shocked?" she asked, a smile playing around her mouth.

"No," he drew the word out a little. "I just thought that... You might say that we're rushing things. When I say we're getting married, I mean we got the marriage license yesterday."

"Well, that is a bit of a surprise, but once you make a decision to do something, there's no point drawing it out." She tilted her head at Kristin. "Unless you wanted a church wedding with all the trimmings?"

"That seems like a waste of money to me. I mean, I guess I'd like some pictures, but I don't want to spend a whole lot of money making one day special, when we can use it for our family."

"You always were pretty practical, and I know Luke will appreciate that about you." Lena's heart was so happy it felt like it might burst. She was thrilled for her son, glad that he had made a good decision. "Did you decide to adopt Becky?" she asked, knowing that it would most likely be possible that her anonymous contact in Lansing could make it go through.

"We're hoping to adopt Becky and perhaps even Rita as well," Kristin said, and there was excitement and hope in her voice.

"I think that might be very doable. I... I guess I didn't expect things to move so quickly, but I have to admit this is not a shock to me."

She didn't try to get them together, but when she heard that Becky had chosen the two of them as parents, it wouldn't have surprised her at all to find out that they came to the conclusion they needed to get married.

"This is kind of anti-climatic. We were confronted by Miss Heather and her friends last night, and I thought that talking to you about it might be just as difficult."

"Did they give you a hard time?" she asked in surprise. She would have thought Kristen's grandma would have been all over this.

"Not really. I guess they just thought we were rushing things too much. I thought that might be what you thought too."

"I think both of you are people who keep your word. I think both of you will give a commitment, and then stand behind it. That's basically what a marriage is. Being able to trust someone to do what they say they're going to do. Of course, it helps when you like that person," she said, smiling as Luke now had his arm around Kristin, and he had pulled her close to his side. It was obvious he wanted her near. That warmed Lena's heart as much as anything.

"I guess maybe we just needed a little push in the right direction, a gentle push, not a shove," Luke said with a grin at Kristin, and they shared a look that said they were both thinking about her gram.

"Sometimes you look at two people and you think that maybe they're a little bit too selfish to make things work, but I think the fact that both of you are willing to put your lives aside in order to take care of Becky, it shows just how selfless you both are. I guess I feel like as long as you keep your word, putting the other person first is probably one of the most important tenets of being married. Where you don't live for yourself, but you live for the people around you. You guys have it down."

"That's a big compliment." Kristin said and she had a lot of respect and appreciation in her tone.

"I will be proud to call you daughter." She smiled a little. "When's the wedding?"

"Tuesday," Luke said, lifting his brows at Kristin like it was something that they talked about, but hadn't decided for sure.

"We figured the sooner the better. We... We'd like to get the girls settled and in school if we can."

"I'll see what I can work out on my end. I had already been given the green light for Becky's adoption if the two of you are married. There had been some chatter about Rita, and I am pretty sure that we can get things worked out. It might not be as quickly as everyone would like, but if you want, I can visit the Cliffords and see if they'll allow Rita to spend several weeks at your house with her sister."

Sometimes it was easier for a third party to negotiate, especially when emotions had a tendency to run high.

"That would be really nice, don't you think?" Luke looked at Kristin.

She nodded. "It didn't sound to me like they care too much about her. But, sometimes people like that will be belligerent just because they can be."

Luke nodded, and turned back to Lena.

"But I don't want you to walk into a dangerous situation. I didn't feel safe at that house. I don't particularly care for the idea of you going there alone."

"I'm not afraid, but I could get someone to go with me. That won't be a problem. I think you're right, sometimes people respond better to a third party and they won't feel like you're trying to get away with anything."

"As foster parents, they know that there will eventually be people interested in adoption. So this shouldn't come as a surprise."

"I agree. I just wish that there were some way that we can keep them from fostering more children. Unfortunately, the system is so stressed that sometimes people slip through the cracks."

Luke and Kristin looked at each other, almost as though they had talked about that, or maybe they were thinking about whether they should consider adopting more children.

"Have you spent much time with the two girls together?" Lena asked, knowing from experience that sometimes having children was endless days of work and mediating arguments.

"Yesterday. But it wasn't too hard."

"Sometimes it's easy, sometimes it feels like it's impossible. But, the days pass by, and soon they're over."

She couldn't believe that her children were all adults already. It felt like the years slipped by and all of a sudden she looked in the mirror and she saw an old lady, when she still felt young inside.

Luke and Kristin smiled at each other, and he seemed confident, which just made Lena shake her head. When she was young, she felt like she knew a good bit, and the older she got, the less she felt like she actually did know. The more she realized she had a lot to learn.

Maybe that would be the way things would go with them.

In the meantime, she was going to do everything in her power to make sure that Becky and Rita had parents who loved them, and Luke and Kristin were perfect for those two little girls.

Chapter 18

“I hate him. He’s ugly. Get him away from me!” Becky slammed the door behind her as she went storming out of the house. She didn’t even stop as she flew by Kristen, who was walking up the steps.

“Hey, kiddo. What’s up?” Luke asked, as she stomped down the steps beside him.

“That stupid dog. He has hair everywhere, he stinks, and I hate him. If he’s going to live here, I’m not!” She crossed her arms over her chest, and finished stomping down the steps.

“Okay,” Luke said, his eyes going to Kristin’s and his brows lifting in inquiry, like he wasn’t quite sure how to handle that.

Kristin had no idea either.

If it was her child who had been brought up in her home, she would immediately jump on that as disrespect, and say that she had been taught better, and she would not speak like that to her dad. But, Luke wasn’t her dad, Becky hadn’t grown up in their house, and their hold on her was tenuous at best. She didn’t have the authority...well, she had the authority, but she didn’t have heart strings tied tight enough in order for her to correct Becky in that manner.

Kristin watched until Becky threw herself in the tent, then, satisfied she wasn’t going to leave the house and go somewhere they couldn’t find her, she turned toward the door, her hand on the knob. Maybe one of the ladies could fill her in on what happened but, as soon as she opened the door, crying spilled out of the house, and Kristin figured that Becky's words had hurt Rita's feelings.

Except, as they walked in and took in the scene in the living room, Rita's black eye said that more than Becky's words had hit Rita.

All right. This was a little more than she had expected.

"Becky hit me!" Rita gasped, throwing herself into Bruno's fur, and sobbing even louder, sounding like her heart was broken and her world had fallen apart."I want to go home!" she wailed.

That struck fear into Kristin's heart and her eyes flew to Luke's. This was supposed to be their home. They *were* home. Not the Cliffords. She wasn't supposed to want to threaten to go back.

"Sweetheart, what happened? Can you tell me?" she said, kneeling beside Rita and putting a tentative hand on her shoulder.

Rita jerked herself away and held tighter to her dog. The poor animal looked like he was used to being cried on, and gave a long-suffering sigh, lifting worried eyes at his mistress before he put his head back down on his front paws, the crease between his brows deep and big.

"The girls were fighting the whole time this morning since I got up. We couldn't even get them to eat breakfast," Gram said, perched on the edge of the couch, like her old legs just couldn't keep her up on her feet anymore.

"Everything we tried just wasn't good enough. Becky found something to bicker about no matter what we did." Joyce crossed her arms over her chest, like she was afraid that Kristin and Luke were going to blame her for the argument. Or maybe for the black eye.

"Did Becky hit you?" Kristin asked, clenching her hand into a fist so she didn't touch the little girl again. She wanted to scoop her up into her arms, but she didn't want to push in when the child obviously didn't trust her. And didn't want her to.

"She almost did!" Rita wailed.

There was a lot more sobbing, before Miss Alma was able to say, "If you're talking about the black eye, it's not because of Becky. Not really. They were fighting over the pancakes we made for breakfast, and Becky yanked her plate away from Rita, which threw Rita off balance, and she took a step forward but tripped over her dog and her face hit the chair."

Kristin couldn't help it. She put a hand to her chest. Part in relief that Becky really hadn't hit her sister, part in horror at how bad that must have hurt.

No wonder Rita was crying and irritable. She'd been through a lot. And, with her beloved sister being angry over her dog...

She probably wasn't angry Kristin thought with a flash of insight.

She was most likely jealous.

"I'm not sure who we should try to handle first," she said, looking at Luke, hoping that he would have some thoughts.

"I'm not so good with tears. Maybe I can handle anger better."

Kristin straightened, and went over to Luke, reaching up to his ear so that Rita couldn't hear what she was going to say.

"I don't think she's angry. I think she's jealous...of the dog of all things. I mean, she's the big sister, and she's used to her little sister idolizing her, but Rita loves her dog, and maybe Becky can't handle it?"

"Good thought," Luke said, nodding. "I think maybe I can try to talk to her?"

"All right. I'll see what I can do here." She gave a wobbly smile and leaned into Luke as he put his arm around her.

"No one said it was going to be easy. And, we'll just do our best. That's all we can do."

She nodded. She knew he was right. No one expected them to be perfect, not even themselves, and she had to remember that. She could only do her best.

Lord. Please help me to say the right thing.

Chapter 19

"What a day," Luke said as he stood at the top of the stairs with Kristen, Becky and Rita finally quiet and in bed for the evening.

Luke had been able to talk to Becky, with Kristin's insight, which was correct. Becky had admitted to feeling jealousy. Once Kristin mentioned it, it was obvious to him that was the problem.

They set up some parameters for Bruno, which didn't miraculously solve any problems, but it did make Becky a little easier to work with. Once she felt that her sister's attention wasn't solely on the dog, she got a little less belligerent.

Rita, for her part, didn't want to leave her beloved pooch, but Kristin was able to get her up and have her sit on her lap while Kristin leaned against the couch and Rita fell asleep.

Luke suspected that perhaps Rita hadn't slept very well the night before because of being out in the tent, and she was just tired and fussy and was clinging to the one thing that was familiar to her. Bruno.

Even her sister, Becky, hadn't been there for her as much as her dog had.

"I have a feeling that... It might not be the hardest day we ever have," Kristin said, and she sounded a little fearful.

"It's not too late for you to back out." Nothing had been set in stone. Yet. He hadn't heard from his mom, and they still had several days until the wedding. "Once we say the vows, it's going to be a little harder to quit."

"I don't want to quit." Her voice was firm, and it held conviction. He was proud of her.

He walked closer, putting his arms around her, and she leaned into his chest, hugging his waist and resting her head on his shoulder.

"We're just getting started."

"Okay. That wasn't very reassuring," she laughed, and he smiled along with her. He supposed it wasn't.

Would they ever be a normal family?

Probably not. There was a lot of pain between the two girls, and he and Kristin weren't exactly getting married in a normal way either.

"Is this too crazy to work?"

"I would say yes, except…I just feel like it's the way the Lord wants us to go. Nothing God does is too crazy to work."

He moved his hand down Kristin's back, and nodded to himself. She was exactly right. If God was in it, it might not work out exactly the way he thought it should, but it would work out exactly the way God wanted it to. And, in the grand scheme of things, that was what really mattered.

"I think the horse ride this evening was exactly what everyone needed. There's just something calming about being on the beach. And horses make it even better." He believed that with his whole soul. He was glad he had asked if the whole family wanted to go down and help them feed the horses, which had led to everyone taking a ride.

He and Kristin talked for a little more, but she was tired, and he encouraged her to go to bed.

For him, he walked slowly home, leaving his truck along the street at Kristin's house. He had promised Becky that she could help him feed the horses in the morning, so he planned to be there early.

It turned out that he didn't sleep very well, and found himself walking the streets at four o'clock in the morning. Way too early for anyone to be up, except as he got closer to Kristin's house, he saw a shadow moving on the sidewalk toward him.

He thought at first it was an animal, and was a little dismayed that he didn't have a weapon. Not that he would want to be shooting a gun off on the streets at that hour of the morning, but if he needed it for self-defense, he certainly would.

Except, there really shouldn't be any animals in the area that would pose any problem to him.

The thought was in and out of his head, before he realized it was a person.

A small person.

A person who was exactly Becky-sized.

She saw him a good thirty seconds after he figured out who she was.

She gasped.

He put his hand on the gate that led to Kristin's house. Maybe she expected him to open it, because she didn't look up, just stared at his fingers.

But he didn't move.

"Interesting time of the day for you to be out taking a walk. Did you let Kristin know where you were going?" His voice was quiet and calm.

"Why should I? She's not my mom."

He pressed his lips together, pursing them and pulling them back. Becky was correct. Kristin wasn't her mom.

"She is the adult in charge of you. Don't you think it would be a courtesy to let her know?"

Becky paused, his appeal to her higher reasoning seemed to floor her. She was ready for a fight, and he hadn't given her one.

"I guess so," she said, although she didn't sound convinced.

"Do you want to tell me where you were?"

"No."

Interesting. If she were just out walking, why wouldn't she say so? So she must have been somewhere. Where could a young teenager have been all night?

"How long have you been out?" Maybe she was just taking a walk.

"I left around midnight."

Four hours. She had been out for four hours.

"Did it occur to you that maybe you should... Check with someone before you just walk around at night?" His words were still calm; he wasn't angry, although... Her calm demeanor and her attitude that she hadn't done anything wrong had stumped him.

His mom would flip out if she caught him walking home at four o'clock in the morning after being out since midnight.

Becky hadn't had a normal home life, he reminded himself.

"No." Her word was said without an attitude. Just a casual no.

"I think maybe that might be something good for you to remember. That, as long as you're here with Kristin and I, if you want to go somewhere, you need to ask permission. And you can't leave in the middle of the night. Not unless you've gotten permission and we told you you could, but... Unless the house is on fire, I really don't think that's going to happen."

She stared down at the ground, not saying anything. He waited, wondering if she was going to agree with him, or if she was going to argue.

It turned out she didn't do either.

"Becky?"

"Are you mad?" She squinted up at him.

"No. I just care about you. I don't know too many good things that happened between midnight and four AM. I know a lot of bad things that do, though. And part of the job of a parent is to protect their children from bad things. That's what God does for us. He gives us rules, boundaries, that protect us from the bad things in life. Sometimes we don't understand those rules and boundaries, but God knows, because God can see things that we can't. That's the same way parents are with their children. Adults can see things the kids can't. That's why they give them boundaries."

"I guess I'm not used to having parents." She kicked her foot on the ground. "There aren't too many people who care about me."

"You're gonna have to get used to it, because it doesn't matter what happens, Kristin and I are always going to care about you." He meant that whether or not they got custody, Becky was in his heart and soul, and he might not have any authority to do anything with her or to her, but he would always care about her.

She probably wouldn't understand that, and he didn't bother to try to explain.

"I can take care of myself," she said, and while her words were a little defiant, her tone was not. "But Rita needs people to look after her."

"Maybe you do too. Maybe you just don't realize it."

She lifted a shoulder.

"I'd like for you to tell me that you won't go out without letting Kristin or I know about it."

"I can't do that. Not until next week."

He let that sink in. So, whatever she was doing…he suspected maybe she was meeting someone. Maybe she needed to tell that person that she wasn't going to meet with them anymore.

Could he give her that much leeway?

"I guess I would prefer you just agreed to do it now."

"I can't."

"But you'll do it next week?"

"Yeah."

"All right." Was he going to just let it go? Yeah, he thought he was. For now. But he'd be watching, now that he knew. "You must be pretty tired."

"Not really." She didn't elaborate, and he didn't ask anything else. He simply opened the gate, and she walked in. He followed her, closing it carefully behind him, and watching as she opened the door without making a noise, and slipped inside. He sat down on the step. He didn't know what Kristin and he were going to do about this new development, but he had to talk to her about it.

After yesterday, he wasn't sure if she would be up for more.

She had to be. This was what they were signing up for.

<h1 style="text-align:center">Chapter 20</h1>

"You take this woman to be your lawfully wedded wife?"

The preacher's voice droned on, and Kristin tried to breathe. It felt like her lungs were frozen, or missing. She wasn't sure which.

The last five days had been a whirlwind. Pretty much at least once a day the girls had had some kind of major fight.

At least Becky didn't seem to have gone out in the middle of the night again. But, she hadn't promised not to either.

Lena had managed to get special permission for them to expedite the process to become foster parents. They had two days of training scheduled later this week, and they'd had to get character witnesses from ten different people in the town.

Character witnesses hadn't been hard, and after what Kristin had been through with the children, she was actually looking forward to the training. Maybe they would have some answers as to how to keep her kids from fighting.

Except, she knew that it was a normal thing. Lena had assured her that kids fought, they made up, and it helped them learn coping skills, people skills, and social skills.

Still, it was stressful and difficult, along with the fact that her gram had been diagnosed as having cancer. A lymphoma-type cancer that doctors thought should be easily treated, as long as it was the kind that responded to treatment. They were testing for that now.

God had been with her through it all, and the man standing in front of her had been solid as a rock. She wasn't sure if she would have survived the last five days without him. She knew for a fact she wouldn't want to be marrying anyone else.

"I do," she said as the pastor waited for her response.

She stood with confidence. She might feel scared to death inside, but that had nothing to do with Luke. If anything, Luke made her feel grounded. There was no doubt in her mind that marrying Luke was one of the best decisions she'd ever made.

On her sane days, she knew that adopting the girls was another decision that had only come because of the Lord.

Just because she felt overwhelmed and incapable of doing the task in front of her, didn't mean that it wasn't God's will for her to keep doing the best she could.

Wasn't that part of what the sacrifice was supposed to be? She gave up the relative calm of her previous life, so that she could work as hard as she could to help these girls. Her eyes slipped to them sitting in the front pew. They didn't have a whole lot of people at their wedding, just Luke's brothers and sisters, the older ladies who lived with her, and Lena of course. Along with the preacher.

Rita had wanted to take Bruno, and she'd shed some tears both in sorrow and in anger when she hadn't been allowed.

Bruno's expulsion had made Becky feel good, and Becky had been acting like the perfect older sister all day.

While it was far from certain that they would be able to eventually adopt the children, fostering them was almost a given, as long as they made it through the special training that they faced later that week.

Lena had said that her anonymous contact had been abundantly clear that this was very unusual, but because of the burden to the system, and because of the girls' special circumstances, they had made special arrangements.

"I now pronounce you man and wife. You may kiss your bride," the preacher intoned.

This was the part she'd been looking forward to. She smiled, only partially in relief. Mostly in anticipation. Luke returned that look, and while their kiss was short and sweet, it held a lot of promises, both promises she gave, and promises she knew he was giving to her.

It was the perfect seal of their vows.

"I love you," Luke whispered as he lifted his head and looked into her eyes.

Her heart felt like it was going to burst. "I love you too." Her words were soft, but she said them with her whole heart. She loved this man, and she knew that while the life they had chosen to make for themselves was not going to be easy, they would face it side-by-side. That was everything she could ever ask.

"Thank you for being willing to walk with me. Share your life with me. I... I think I'll look back on this day as the best day of my life. It sure feels that way."

She didn't think he could have said anything more romantic to her.

"I can't believe I'm married to the best man in the entire world. I'm looking forward to the challenge." That was mostly true. The part about him being the best man in the world was absolutely true. And most of the time she was looking forward to the challenge.

"And when we can't take the challenge anymore, we'll have the beach and the horses and the sunset, and God will reset our hearts, and give us the strength we need to keep going. I'm sure of it."

She nodded, because she knew he was right. Whatever they were facing, God was with them, and that was really all they needed to find joy in their hearts.

Epilogue

Griff wiped his hands on his apron and set his spatula down. Luke and Kristen had just walked in the diner and he wanted to go out and congratulate them. Word had already reached the diner that they'd been approved as foster parents to Becky and Rita and he figured they were here to celebrate.

Griff had already made a strawberry crunch pound cake he intended to give them for dessert, but he didn't carry it out with him as he walked from the kitchen to the dining area.

Chi had been taking an order from a table in the back, but she'd come out too when she'd heard the new family come in. She caught his eye as they walked toward Luke and Kristen who stood at the door, like they were discussing where to sit.

Chi wore a smile, which made Griff's heart warm like it always did. Her smiles had been fewer and farther between lately. Griff suspected that had something to do with the lawyer she seemed to favor, but she hadn't said and he hadn't asked. Maybe he should, but he'd moved on the property they'd wanted to move the diner to instead. That was probably a typical male move - rather than talk to her, he did something he thought would make her very happy. And, at the same time, would hopefully get her mind off the lawyer as she focused on moving the diner and turning the currently-empty building into something successful.

"Hey! We heard the happy news! Congratulations!" Chi reached forward and grabbed Kristen, giving her a hug.

Griff held his hand out to Luke. "I'm happy for you, man," he said. It didn't escape his notice that it appeared that Chi and he were side-by-side, congratulating the couple together like they'd planned it, or like they were together. He'd never felt a connection with anyone like he felt with Chi. Like they were linked together somehow without words.

But Chi did not seem to feel the same way.

"We're thrilled that we passed the training and have our fostering certification," Luke said. "But we're even more thrilled that Becky and Rita are ours and we're one step closer to being a family."

"Where's your gram and the other ladies?" Chi asked, standing back, but still holding both of Kristen's hands in hers, squeezing and sharing Kristen's happiness.

"They're planning a little celebration at home tomorrow." She bit her lip and looked at Griff. "I was wondering if you might have time to make a cake for us? I know it's last minute..."

"I already have a strawberry crunch cake sitting on top of the fridge to send home with you. If you want something more, I'd be happy-"

"That's perfect!" Kristen beamed.

Griff noticed that she looked at Luke and they shared the kind of smile that people in love often shared. His heart squeezed a bit, not out of jealousy, but maybe just sorrow that it would never be him having the woman he loved look at him like that - like he was an important part of her world. No, like he *was* her world.

They chatted a bit more with Luke and Kristen and their kids before they walked over to a booth by the window and sat down.

"I'm so happy for them," Chi murmured as they left.

"Me too." He almost added that Kristen and Luke were perfect for each other, even though it had taken them a while to figure that out. Actually, it had taken Luke a while to figure it out mostly because he was so busy resisting Kristen's gram that he didn't have time to actually look at Kristen.

But he didn't say anything. Not just because that wasn't something men typically said, but because he felt that Chi was so busy looking at her lawyer that she couldn't see the man who loved her and was perfect for her right in front of her face.

"Thanks for making a cake for them," Chi said as she turned, stuffing her note pad in her pocket.

"I'll pay for it," he said.

"Don't worry about it. I was going to give them their meals, too. It's the least we can do to help them celebrate."

The diner was barely breaking even, and Chi had very little money. It was a huge sacrifice for her to offer to give four free meals. But Griff just nodded, loving her generous heart. She never made a big deal about the things she gave to the community and she never complained about money, but he saw it. Chi didn't know and didn't want him to see, he was sure. But when a man loved a woman, he wanted to know everything about her.

Or maybe it was her generous heart that made him love her to begin with. The line was murky and Griff didn't figure it was necessary to figure it out. He just wanted Chi to notice the same things about him.

But she didn't.

He turned and followed her back to the counter, slipping behind it and walking back to his spot in the kitchen. He'd be able to tell her soon about the properties he bought. Hopefully, she'd be just as happy and excited as he thought she would be. Happy and excited enough to put the lawyer out of her head.

Griff could only hope.

Enjoy this preview of *There I Find Trust,* just for you!

Chapter 1

"Congratulations on your new property." Michael Flanagan shook Griff Deant's hand. "I don't understand why you want to live up there in the middle of nowhere, but I'm happy for you, man. You deserve a little peace."

Griff grinned like he was supposed to and said some words of appreciation to his longtime friend and buddy.

They'd grown up together, Michael and he, although Griff had taken a few detours before he'd gotten to where Michael had gone straight as an arrow.

After he'd gotten there, Griff had realized that the white-collar life wasn't for him.

That didn't keep him from working hard, and most people would say he had gotten lucky.

He would have said that God smiled on him.

Regardless, he'd gotten himself out of the rat race as quickly as he could, although he hadn't planned on settling down in Strawberry Sands.

"I've never owned a beach house before. So it's a first."

"I think that's the thing with successful lawyers in Chicago. We all have beach houses."

"Well, I'm no longer a successful lawyer in Chicago, so maybe I'm a little late to the party, but I got here."

"Being late to the party seems to be the story of your life. I've never seen anyone take so much garbage and turn it into gold the way you have. Usually drug addiction sinks a man faster than a stone." Michael shook his head, slapped Griff on the back, and they exited the big conference room together. It wasn't like they needed all that area. There had been stacks and reams of paper to sign, but it'd only been Flanagan and himself in the room.

What would Chi say?

He found himself asking that question in his mind over and over again since he started working at her diner several years ago.

He didn't know why, since Chi didn't seem to give a flip what he thought, even though he couldn't seem to get her out of his mind. It was the first time in his life where he truly understood the meaning of unrequited love. Unfortunately, most of the town of Strawberry Sands knew exactly how he felt. Even worse, they knew exactly how Chi felt.

At least it was a small town.

"How about lunch?" Michael said as they walked to the reception area together.

"I'll pass. I'm got a couple-hour drive up to Strawberry Sands yet, and now that I have the key to my property, I think I'd like to get settled in. We've got that winter storm coming."

Michael slapped him on the back once more, understanding that it wasn't a personal thing for him to turn the dinner invitation down.

Griff had always done better by himself anyway. Because of the things he'd experienced, he just wasn't like everyone else. Strawberry Sands suited him much better than Chicago. Maybe even being a short-order cook matched his personality better than being a corporate lawyer.

None of it was very satisfying. Possibly because there was still something in his soul that just wasn't filled.

Not that Jesus wasn't enough. He was. There was just...a disquiet he couldn't seem to shake.

Maybe that was the way everyone felt and no one ever talked about it.

He considered that on his way north toward his new hometown.

He'd been living in an apartment over the diner since he arrived in Strawberry Sands, and he was content there. But it wasn't every day that a man had the opportunity to purchase a beach house a ten-minute walk from where he worked.

The only thing that kept Griff from jumping on it to begin with was the fact that he didn't want to purchase it alone. He wanted Chi beside him. And if she didn't like it, they'd look until they found one that she did.

The one he just purchased was a little pretentious, definitely bigger than he would ever need as a single man. But he could dream. Maybe it would be filled up with children at some point. And a wife. He definitely wanted a wife. Although not just anyone. Maybe some men could go around and find any pretty face that would do, but he wasn't really interested in pretty faces. He...could only seem to get himself interested in Chi.

Of course, the second property he'd just bought held a lot more hope that Chi would be excited about it.

In fact, he could barely wait to tell her about it.

Maybe he drove just a little faster than he should have on his way north, because of the excitement of that second property. It was much less expensive than the first, much smaller, and not nearly as nice, but it was the one he knew would make Chi smile.

He wasn't sure when it happened, when making Chi smile had become one of his focuses in life. In fact, perhaps the main focus, other than making food for the diner. Especially strawberry recipes. Of course, the bottom line with that was making Chi smile as well. After all, if his strawberry recipes brought people into the diner, that definitely made Chi happy.

It was almost too cold for him to ride his bike, but the leather kept most of the chill out as he pulled off the interstate and took a two-lane toward the beach.

He hadn't told Chi what he was doing, just that he would be late for work this morning. He was never late, and he never missed; this was only the second time in the years he'd been working for her that he hadn't been there if the diner was open.

Even snow didn't keep him away, considering his apartment was just above the diner.

As he motored into town, he noticed there seemed to be more people than usual at the diner.

That wasn't necessarily a good thing. He didn't like taking a morning off and having the place get busier. That didn't say a lot for his popularity.

But he wasn't worried. He knew the food he made was good. He knew the recipes he made were popular, and he knew they helped make a place for him in Strawberry Sands, enabled him to give back to the community and to try to make up for the beginning of his life which had been a lot more take than give.

He'd made up everything that he needed to yesterday in order to have the special be easy for Chi to put together on this chilly, early December day, with dark gray clouds overhead and water that reflected the sky's mood.

He loved how Lake Michigan changed with the weather and the seasons and with a mind of its own.

He'd been fascinated with the lake since he first saw it, and while the house he bought might be a little ostentatious, he finally closed on a place where he could look out from almost any window in his house and see what she was doing at that very moment.

He parked his bike along the sidewalk, chilled to the bone.

He wasn't used to driving the whole way to Chicago, and if he made a habit of it, he'd have to get a regular vehicle.

Michigan was not suited for motorcycles from about October to April. Thankfully they were in the middle of an unseasonably warm spell which was supposed to usher in a huge snowstorm along with a massive swing downward in temps.

Still, he was partial to his old roadster and normally did not spend a lot of money.

It took a bit to get in the door of the diner, talking to the patrons and chatting about the weather, town life, and pretty much anything. Everyone was familiar, and everyone was a friend.

It felt odd though, like there was something going on that he couldn't quite put his finger on. Like people were holding something back from him. It was a strange sensation, but he felt like that more than once when people stopped talking midsentence and then changed the subject quickly.

Normally just as they were talking about Chi. Odd.

He made his way to the counter, then stepped behind and walked to the back. He saw Chi take a load of dishes back, and he figured he'd stick his apron on and start cooking as soon as he washed his hands. But he really wanted to share his news with her. This seemed like a good day to share it with the community as well, since there were so many people in the dining area, and it wasn't even lunchtime.

"Hey there," he said as he stepped in. Chi's back was to him as she moved the dishes off her tray and onto the counter by the sink.

"You're back. That's great." She barely smiled at him as she turned around, grabbing her tray.

"I am." He kind of wanted to tell her at a special time. To have the two of them together, talking, so he could surprise her with his good news, but the way she seemed so distracted, like she didn't even care whether he'd come back or not, bothered him, and maybe he wanted her attention, which was why the words slipped out without any type of fanfare.

"I bought the piece of property at the end of the street. The one where we talked about moving the diner. Where patrons can go out on the patio and eat with the great views of Lake Michigan."

That was a lot more than he normally said. He'd learned from a young age to keep his mouth shut and his eyes open. But he rambled just a bit, because his words didn't even make Chi stop moving. She had been throwing the garbage away, scraping off plates, and checking the food on the stove.

As soon as he was done, she spoke, not even looking at him.

"I told everyone today, and you might as well know too. I'm closing the diner."

Griff knew he was supposed to say something. This was a conversation and was his turn to talk. But his mouth wouldn't move. It had fallen open, and he couldn't close it.

Chi grabbed the rag along with the pan of water, shoving her tray under her arm, and began to walk past him.

"You're closing the diner?"

He'd just bought property. Planned to stay. To help her move the diner where they'd talked about.

"You mean you're closing it in order for us to move?" It was a question, but he tried to say it like a statement. Like he knew what she was talking about.

"No. Like I'm closing it down and moving to Chicago. The lawyer that I've been seeing has invited me to move in with him, and I've accepted."

He blinked. Then blinked again, his mouth still feeling frozen in an "O" position.

She was going to move in with the dude?

That wasn't Chi. She wasn't like that. Of course, he knew that was typical. People did it all the time, but Chi was different. She had morals and values and standards, and she tried to live by them.

"When?"

"Today's my last day." She spoke simply, like she didn't just explode his world with the other statement she made, and that she hadn't totally taken his job. Usually there was at least a two-week notice.

Although, he knew there were times where owners just didn't show up for work anymore, and a closed sign in the evening ended up being permanent.

But he never thought that would happen here.

"I was going to offer to sell this to you, but I guess if you've already bought the property at the end of the street, you won't want this one. I'll be putting it up for sale, so make sure you get any personal items out at the end of the day."

Right. His personal items.

What about his heart? She didn't understand that it was right here in the kitchen with them, in her possession. When she walked out, moving in with her high-dollar, fancy lawyer from Chicago, she'd be taking it with her. He wished he could stop her, but that wasn't exactly something he had control over.

"Actually, if things slow down this afternoon, I'll be closing early. So just wanted to let you know," she said, and then she breezed out of the kitchen.

Griff stood silent, his chest heaving up and down. She was leaving. Closing the diner. Moving in with another man.

That was the thing.

Closing the diner, he could handle. He didn't need this job.

Leaving might be a little harder, but if she were leaving to open a diner somewhere else or even get a job somewhere else, he could handle that as well.

But moving in with another man? And that slimy, big-city lawyer, who was a crook and a cheat if Griff had ever seen one. And he'd seen plenty.

But he couldn't tell that to Chi. She wouldn't listen. She wasn't interested in his opinion on who she dated or...apparently who she moved in with.

He swallowed, wondering if there was any point in even walking over to the stove and getting started at the job he loved.

He loved it because of Chi. Although, he definitely found a solace and a certain type of relaxation and contentment in cooking. In feeding people. In making things that they loved and ate and enjoyed. Making people smile, but most of all Chi.

Griff stood staring at the door, discouraged and heartsick where he had spent the last few hours excited about the news he had, and now that it had been a letdown, he looked over where he'd stood for so many hours at the stove, working, because he enjoyed it, true, but mostly because of Chi.

He had one day left, but it didn't matter. If she hadn't noticed him all the other days that he'd been there, today wasn't going to be any different. Why stay?

Because that's what a man of character did.

Pick up your copy of *There I Find Trust* by Jessie Gussman today!

A Gift from Jessie

View this code through your smart phone camera to be taken to a page where you can download a FREE ebook when you sign up to get updates from Jessie Gussman! Find out why people say, "Jessie's is the only newsletter I open and read" and "You make my day brighter. Love, love, love reading your newsletters. I don't know where you find time to write books. You are so busy living life. A true blessing." and "I know from now on that I can't be drinking my morning coffee while reading your newsletter – I laughed so hard I sprayed it out all over the table!"

Claim your free book from Jessie!

www.ingramcontent.com/pod-product-compliance
Lightning Source LLC
Chambersburg PA
CBHW070514200726
48293CB00007B/2533